Cold Daughters

by

Diana Johnson

Diana Johnson

To:
Snara
Enjoy the Story.
Merry Christmas!
Always
Diana

ISBN-13: 978-1-6923-1197-1

For Kenton, my hero.

CONTENTS

Acknowledgments

1	United Coalition December 21, 2040	1
2	Nia December 22, 2027	8
3	Ahi 2028	22
4	Happy Birthday!	38
5	Barrett and Ahi 2032	54
6	Nia and Hope 2032	70
7	Quantum Biology 2037	76
8	The Evolution 2040	85
9	The Transition 2040	93
10	The Beginning	106
11	The Projects	111
12	The End	142
13	The Solstice	169

Thank you, Deb, Annie, Josh, and Lucas.
You're the best readers and some of the finest people I know.
Your help was invaluable.

United Coalition December 21, 2040

Great Assembly Hall, Belgium

Dr. Claudia Dereksen, renowned geneticist and quantum biologist was ushered to an armchair behind a curved desk, on the stage at the front of the sprawling auditorium. The seats to her left and right were occupied by colleagues and peers of other disciplines all presenting to the United Coalition during this emergency special session. She met the eyes of the others, and with a pointed glance she delivered respect to those she regarded most highly and contempt to the ones she loathed and even blamed for the reasons they gathered that day. The inset monitors were powered up and a white light illuminated the chests and chins of the panelists and refracted in their water glasses. The pallor of the lean scientists stood in stark contrast to the golden, overinflated military men. They each reviewed their own slides as the din in the great hall softened and their audience settled into place. The Secretary General stood before a giant holographic projection screen welcoming representatives from every nation state and the international press corps. His introduction of the panelists was practiced and precise, but his posture could not mask his anxiety. Never in the history of this body had a meeting of this nature taken place. His own covert part in what was about to be revealed could end his tenure as its leader. With the introductions complete,

Commander Merle took the lead.

Claudia listened resentfully to the accomplished chief recapping the maneuvers that created the devastation in the South China Seas nearly fourteen years prior. She reacted viscerally to anyone trying to justify war. Talk of war always stoked the fear of something and she'd rather be in pain than afraid. As he spouted off his political fiction, she could only think of Ahi and how she had worked so hard all her life to help avoid this disaster. And now when they may have found a way to ensure that all would not be lost, *she* would be lost anyway.

Her heart dragged her back to the autumn she began at the English School of The Hague. She was a knobby kneed twelve-year-old in the mid 1970's, starting the sixth grade in the elite academy. Walking home at the end of her third day of classes, a gypsy girl accosted her in the lane beyond the gate. The girl appeared head and shoulders taller and looked dark and dirty and too thin to be well, but Claudia really only remembered *that* as an adult. All she saw in the moment were the girl's desperate green eyes. The gypsy girl warned Claudia that the next night, in that same spot, she would have to pay for safe passage past. Claudia had been cautioned about this "element" around the school but none of her classmates had reported any run-ins. She went home, keeping the incident to herself for fear of appearing unable to manage without help. The only thing she could imagine worse than getting rolled by a traveler was having her governess walk her to school! The next day at school she asked some of the upper classmen about their experiences.

That's when she first met Ahi.

The clump of girls gathered in the hall discussing the threat parted as if they sensed something otherworldly approaching, and there she stood filling the gap they'd left, beautiful brown skin and an inky silk mane falling down around her petite uniform lapel, her black eyes honing in on Claudia's fearful expression.

With her graceful hands clasped around the spines of her senior class texts, she coolly inquired, "What's all this then?" When one of the girls explained Claudia's plight, Ahi simply replied, "I go that way, love. I'll walk with you after class."

Claudia, rapt, simply nodded and watched as the smiling Ahi glided by. She squirmed with anticipation all day and when Miss Janssen dismissed her group, she raced to the gate where the students exited the gardens. The two began their journey down the lane talking as if they'd known each other for a lifetime. And when they came to the bay where the gypsy girl lay in wait, Ahi glanced over her shoulder just long enough to make eye contact with the mongrel and kept right on walking.

Once well past her, Ahi parked Claudia and backed up to the crouching imp and leaned in to discreetly utter through clenched teeth, "If you ever lay a hand on my mate, I will scratch your eyes out." The girl darted away without looking back and Ahi rejoined her charge and delivered her home as if nothing had happened.

Back in the now, Claudia eked a private smile and thought, "I wish you were here to scare the bullies away one last time, my love." While the windy commander was still laying out the positions of the targeted military bases and the connection between the Russians and the North Koreans, Claudia grew more and more defensive listening again ad nauseam, about the regimes responsible for the attack. There were so many tiny territories that were simply erased from the map. She thought that no one would mention the names of the islands that crumbled and sank during the assault and the ones that were covered by the walls of water that erupted with every tsunami that followed it. Maps of the region before and after with nothing but sea where Indonesia and the Philippines used to be created the doomsday drama so expertly orchestrated for centuries by the agents of war. Claudia felt the anger redden her neck and flush over her face. She sat tapping her wedding ring and trying to block out the commander's meanderings about "stopping the carnage before any more damage was wrought." Her eyes returned to her material and she listened only for the wrap up of the 'why?' and waited for the 'now what?' by her colleague from the Helio-Dynamics Observatory.

When Dr. Stanof began her presentation, Claudia softened her grip on her pen and inhaled slowly to calm herself. She was naturally more relaxed when a fellow intellectual was in command of the room. Patiently, she absorbed Dr. Stanof's explanation of the Banda Arc and the Weber Deep. The detonation of the bombs, in the 2027 attack on the military installations in the Philippines furthered the subduction of the tectonic plates in the region, piercing the Earth's mantle to depths that hadn't even been imagined prior to the war. The results at the surface were devastating enough with the tidal damage and volcanic activity but the real damage was the ticking clock that began when the jagged edges of the broken plate created a fault that would interrupt the very conduction of the Earth's heat and magnetic fields. She listened intently to her learned colleague describe the way our planet was largely heated from within, from the inner core of solid iron to the outer core of varying currents of heated and moving and pressurized metals creating a convective, magnetic heating element.

"Our planet's defenses have been compromised with the creation of this rift in the ocean floor. Our daily temperature readings have shown descending patterns which signify two things. First the Earth's core is cooling at an accelerated rate. This has already led to changes in the oceanic currents and brought about socio-economic wreckage to the island states that remain in the area. And secondly and more gravely, the magnetic field that protects this planet from harmful space radiation, chiefly from the sun itself, has weakened and morphed from its usual currents around the Earth."

As the screen behind the doctor exhibited slide after slide of the curving lines representing the planet's fluctuating protective layers before and after the attack, Claudia remembered when these changes were first identified and scientists like herself and Dr. Stanof began laboring in favor of plan after plan to correct the damage. She lamented the time that was wasted on even agreeing with the findings, how so many argued that the rollback was the culprit and not the destruction from the war. As if that somehow had a bearing on how to fix it!

She shook off her negativity and tuned back into the doctor's solar weather predictions that were, indeed, the reason for the assembly today. Stanof and her team had been able to predict with pinpoint accuracy the approach of many solar storms with the helioseismic and magnetic imagers at the observatory. Months ago, following a large collection of flares that destroyed several satellites and one small, unmanned space station, they began tracking the mega storm that would most certainly become a threat to Earth's survival. Deploying a plan of action to correct the damaged area in the Pacific would be the only defense against the impending threat. We had to act now to repair the fissure in the ocean floor and restore the strength of the magnetic field around the Earth. The Southern Hemisphere would be in perfect position at the height of the winter solstice for the devastation the doctor was warning about.

"But I am here today to inform you that with our magnetic field in its current state of flux, the radiation from the imminent solar storm will reach our atmosphere and it will destroy the Earth. We have no other defense against the sun's harmful radiation. The troposphere will ignite, searing the planet's surface. Areas that are not immediately destroyed by fire will be uninhabitable second to the toxic gases produced by the incineration of the megatons of plastic and petroleum deposits everywhere on the planet." Stanof delivered the warning with perfect poise; factual, clean, and terrifying.

Claudia took a sip from her water glass and prepared to begin her presentation as the doctor concluded, "With the world's most sharply trained minds searching the globe for anything that could inspire a remedy, and thirteen years of mechanical apparatus either disabled on land or sunken in the South China Seas in failure, we've turned to a colleague of mine who's research into the connection between fundamental physics and human consciousness has brought about The Solstice Project. Dr. Claudia Dereksen."

Nia December 22, 2027

Huffman Children's Research Institute, Victoria, Australia

Alone in her darkened office, Dr. Nia Bomani stared into the illuminated bank of films displayed on her wall and dictated an updated note on her latest patient. "Baby Djalu diagnostic results – semicolon – MRI of brain without contrast and CT of brain without contrast and laboratory markers of hormonal levels all consistent with increased activity of the pineal gland – period. No other glandular over activity – period. No evidence of mass or malformation to support leukocoric appearance of right eye – period. Objective findings from daily vitals reveal normal heart rate – comma – respirations – comma – color – comma - and reflexes – period. Patient remains hypothermic with an average sustained body temperature of 28 degrees Celsius – comma - with no apparent adverse effects – period. Patient's parents struggling with social issues related to ophthalmic abnormalities – parentheses – right heterochromia iridium with sectoral abnormality and leukocoria - parentheses - subsequently mother refusing to breast feed and-slash-or otherwise bond counter to nursing staff education – period. Social work consult answered but no note from that department as of the time of this dictation - period." A knock at the door broke her concentration and produced the flash of familiar irritability that always accompanied the many interruptions in her days at the Institute. "Come."

“Excuse me, Dr. Bomani,” began the tiny silhouetted figure of a woman as she entered the dim room, “Karri Colebee, Genetic Support Network, I was called by your social worker in regard to the Djalu infant. Do you have a moment?”

“I was just reviewing her tests, Ms. Colebee, yes come in, please.” Nia swiped her screen down and the lights up and genuinely focused her intent in the direction of her guest. “I must say I’m surprised to know that you’ve been brought in for this baby. I felt like this was a clear case of superstition on the part of these young parents and I was sure our in-house group would be able to handle it with education. What’s happened? Fill me in.”

“Well, doctor, when I spoke to the folks in social work, the parents were already asking for adoption options…yesterday…just after she was born! The team downstairs thought that bigger guns were necessary to help inform and support this family. But I’m afraid the lot of us has been unable to allay their fears.”

“I know this hypothermia is perplexing and the one blue eye with the white, key-hole pupil is a little shocking at first, but this baby girl is perfectly healthy otherwise. I have initiated contact with my mentor from Oxford regarding this patient in an effort to shed some light on her unique condition. She is truly the most interesting baby I’ve met. Have you seen her?”

“I requested an observation visit with first mom and baby, then dad and baby, then the triad and quite frankly the baby was the most, well-adjusted of the three." Colebee referenced her notes and continued, "It seems that this baby girl was conceived just after the South China Sea attacks and her parents saw that event as a resurgence of the Aboriginal Dreamtime. They believe that even if she didn't physically come out of those displaced tectonic plates, that she at least has some supernatural connection to that event. They fear that her birth has upset the laws of existence and they fear the child herself."

"I know the Aboriginal lore is sacred but we're nearly a third of the way through the twenty-first century for Christ's sake! Surely we can do more to educate and inform." The usual professional distance Nia put between herself and her patient-families felt surprisingly thin with this case. "She's just remarkably alert and interactive for a newborn," she bragged. A buzz of her earpiece prompted her to answer, "Nia Bomani." She held Ms. Colebee at bay with a raised finger then completed the call. "We'll be right down."

"Is it the Djalu's?" asked Colebee.

"They've left the clinic…without her."

Ms. Colebee could be heard through the glass walls of the nursery, interrogating the nurses and support staff gathered in the adjacent station. While they pored over the documents left behind by her parents, Nia stared down at the tiny infant in her acrylic nest, electrodes connected to her hands, feet and head. She opened the layette and carefully removed the infant and cradled her in her arms with a comforting smile. The baby grunted and wriggled. The two looked an unlikely pairing of extremes. Nia with her nappy, short blonde hair, gray-brown, freckled complexion and moss-colored eyes and the orphan she held whose dark skin and swirls of fine, glossy hair as black as pitch framed her unique gaze, one eye onyx and one sky blue.

"There, little dove. There's a good girl. Don't lose hope, darling. That would make a great autograph, *Hope Darling*. We are going to learn so very much from each other. First lesson, you don't always belong to who you came from." The baby lay still and engaged in the arms of her new champion. The bonding had begun. A muted wrapping on the nursery glass raised Nia's eyes toward the nurse's station where another staffer had entered the busy group and stared blankly at her and the infant. "What?"

"Dr. Bomani," he affirmed, muffled from behind the glass, "we have another one."

In the seventy-two hours that followed Hope's admission to the Institute, a total of eighty-three female infants were born to mothers along the northwestern coastal territories of Australia. All born with the same abnormalities as her own, the overactive pineal gland, the cold body temperature and the abnormal color and shape of the right eye. They were all transferred to Nia's care and a P.R. team was flagged to begin communication between the parents and the press. Nia, having not left the Institute in the entirety of those seventy-two hours finally exited her office after finishing rounds at about eleven in the morning, exhausted and anxious.

"You left my number for Dr. Dereksen?" Nia quizzed Marjorie, her assistant of many years.

"Yes Dr. Nia, please get some rest and we'll call you if anything comes up."

"Call me if Hope needs anything. I'll be back in a couple of hours."

Her commute to her apartment on any given day was barely ten minutes even with heavy traffic. With her mind racing and a dangerous level of fatigue she hadn't dealt with since medical school, the trip seemed to take hours that morning. She reached her cluttered living room and collapsed in a heap on the couch, rang the Thai place in the plaza down the block and ordered some curry and rice, then closed her eyes.

She had already begun to dream when the food came. As she shook herself awake to make the exchange at the door, the call came in.

"Thank you," she jammed too much money into the hands of the delivery guy and answered the phone, slinging the take-out to the counter. "Hello, Claudia?"

"So how many have you got?"

"Eighty-three. We had the first one three days ago. When did you hear?"

"Then you've had the first one. I've been getting calls for the last twenty-four hours. They had twenty-six in Jakarta. There have been twenty-four in Surabaya. Waigeo is reporting another two dozen. Thirty-four between East and West Nusa Tenggara and twenty-one in Timor."

Nia abandoned her food and swiped up her computer screen to review a map of the areas, while tallying the count in her head. "That's a total of two-hundred-thirty-three, all across the sea from the Banda Arc…all along the rift from the war. Claudia, what does it mean?"

"I'll be damned if I know, Nia. But that's not all of it," Claudia cautiously lead. "These are only the ones who are making it into clinic. Authorities in Jakarta, Waigeo, and Timor reported finding a total of twenty-one bodies all together since yesterday."

"Oh God! Not witchcraft?"

"Voodoo, witchcraft, superstition. These peoples' lives were upended after those bloody bombs. They were and still are terrified. Some of the babies have been left on the doorsteps of city officials and churches. Not all of these little island nations are progressive enough to handle such uncommon orphans."

"Claudia, we have to do something! These babies can't be left to the barbaric bullshit of these primitive people. The Institute is in the process of waging an all-out blitz of reeducation for our parents and staff. A third of the girls born in our territory were abandoned at the hospitals that delivered them. We've recruited two new groups of social workers to find foster families and called in four more psychologists to work exclusively with our moms and dads. We can't lose any more of these babies to ignorance and fear!" Her eyes were full of hot tears. The fissure in her childhood heart was as deep as the one created by the great bombs and she openly wept for the decades of helplessness she felt.

"Nia," Claudia soothed, "this isn't Tanzania. We will keep them safe. You have to keep your head."

"I'm sorry I'm so emotional." Nia attempted to straighten herself. "I'm just tired. And I need to eat."

"That's an excuse. What's the reason?"

Erupting in tears again, Nia collapsed onto the rug.

"Nia, what is it?" Claudia asked tenderly. "You've worked your whole career taking care of unique children like these. What's got you so upset?

"Not like these, Claud. Not like this one!" she cried.

"Which one?"

"The first one," she sobbed, "they left her, Claudia!" Trying desperately to release the pain in her heart and regain her emotions at the same time, Nia croaked in fits and starts. "They were…afraid…of their own child!"

"Yes, dear, the bastards left her. Heartless, I know."

The young doctor breathed deeply to reset. "Who are these people? Who are they to turn away from their incredible, weird, cold daughter?"

"*Frigus filiae.*"

"What? Is that Latin?"

"*Frigus filiae.* Cold daughters."

"But she is perfect. She is this perfect, other-worldly jewel. And they just left her."

"Say it, Nia. Say what you are trying not to say."

"I want her. Claudia, I want to raise Hope as my own."

"Hope, is it? You've taken the liberty of naming her? Nia, these girls are really different. Before you go off to save them you need to take a step back. Maybe you should call Dan. This is too big a decision not to consult your doctor."

"Claudia, I'm fine. I'm not trying to right any wrongs. I spent years getting over all that, and for the last two I've been on the waiting list for an infant. I've been talking to *you* about doing this. I want this baby girl. The board has assembled a special committee to act as legal guardian of these babies and is fast-tracking adoption circumventing the state agencies to ensure that the girls stay enrolled in our research. So, the process would only take seven to ten days and I could have a daughter of my own."

"Please just call him. It won't hurt to revisit some of your issues to be certain that you are really ready for what this means." Nia sat hushed and judged. "You can tell me all about your session in a couple of days. I'll be in by Friday and after clinic I'll take you shopping. Ahi will insist on getting everything you'll need for the nursery."

The mention of her name brought up a lump in Nia's throat and instant shame that she was going on like a spoiled child. "I'm so sorry, I didn't even ask. How is Ahi?"

"She just received her second opinion and is weighing the options of chemo and surgery. The cancer is stage IV and fairly aggressive, but so is Ahi Mulpuru!" Now the lump was in Claudia's throat. "A baby would be good news for all of us."

"I truly love you two." Nia declared.

"We love you too. Call him!"

Wiping her tears, Nia began to giggle at the thought of her dear friends doting over the beautiful Hope. She sank into the couch again and fell deeply and peacefully asleep.

~

Daniel Roach had an office that opened right out into the hall of the aging building in which it was leased. 'Room 110' was painted on the privacy glass centered over a dirty brass mail slot with a laminated 'Session in progress, please wait' sign looped over the blackened doorknob. The chairs lining the hall were empty and as she approached, Nia discovered that the door was slightly ajar. "Nia, is that you?" Dr. Roach bellowed from within the office.

Peeking around the door, she answered the empty room, "Yes, Dan. Where are you?"

"I'm just finishing up in here," he called from behind the bathroom door. She smiled with a blush of embarrassment for them both and entered the office space, quietly closing the door behind her and depositing her bag on the floor next to the 'patient's' chair. She slowly walked around the warm, rust-colored, shelf-lined chamber admiring the book titles and photos of all the exotic places her psychologist had visited. It had been nearly a year since their last session and some new tchotchkes had taken their place among the odd stones and other trophies of the good doctor's grateful patients' journeys. She barely heard the flush when he erupted from the lavatory, drying his hands on his corduroy slacks. "Nia!" he reached for her with outstretched arms. "Claudia told me you would come. I've missed you." His embrace was crushing and wonderful.

"I've missed you too, Dan." He took a step back but kept hold of Nia's hands. "Thanks for seeing me on such short notice but I really need to talk this out with someone, and you've always given me sound counsel."

"Yes, let's get to it." They sank into the overstuffed, aging leather chairs flanking the old steamer trunk Dr. Roach used as a coffee table and occasionally a net, dividing the court between doctor and patient. "Surely you don't feel the need to dredge up all your past work. So where do we begin?"

"No. I am done struggling with all that pain. Every day that I wake up in my little flat and go off to work with my incredible patients, I thank the universe for surviving my childhood. I relinquish my survivor's guilt for not being terrorized like my sister. And I renew my compassionate state of forgiveness for both my parents for their role in what happened to her. Dan, all I have to do is look at the accomplishments of my lifetime since my own rescue, to see that I've made good use of the chances I was given to live and thrive. I've done all this *for* my sister and all the other children who were lost or scarred and *despite* my feelings of betrayal and abandonment." Dr. Roach listened to Nia with a smile creeping onto his face and as she heard herself and continued, she was smiling as well. “Ok. I hear it. I guess I did need to take a little inventory first. I practically recited my whole gratitude mantra for you just now.”

“This is good,” he chuckled. “You are so thorough in everything you do, Nia. I wouldn’t expect anything else.”

“Right. But today, Dan, I have overcome this prejudice. And who better to take on a child who is facing a similar bias? Some of these babies have already been killed. Most of them have been abandoned and we can’t even be sure that the ones who remain in the care of their parents are safe.”

“Mmm-hm. Claudia told me that they are truly unique. Tell me about the little one you’ve become attached to.”

“Her name is Hope and she is magical. You’ve read of course about the eyes and the cold temperatures?” He nodded as she continued, “But I’m really enthralled with the pineal gland over-activity.”

“Yes, I’ve studied the pineal gland’s mystical place in the world’s major religions. Some maintain that its production of Dimethyltryptamine gives us the ability to join our consciousness in otherworldly ways to planes of another existence. Shaman and yogis around the world have taught their followers how to connect with and use this gland and its hormonal activity to obtain vision beyond our senses and psychic abilities. Perhaps the *Frigus Filiae* have been endowed with some of these same gifts."

"There's been no evidence of any psychic abilities. And frankly, it's that kind of speculation that has people in their own communities, their own families viewing these girls as a threat. We have no idea what it means."

"I'd caution you that you have no idea what it means for them, for their quality of life or their mortality. Nia, what if they were only meant to remain for a season? How could you manage that grief?"

She let the question sink in. It's not like she hadn't thought about it already. How long could any infant with such a low body temperature survive and to what levels could they develop? Even though none of the girls were experiencing any problems yet, no one could predict their life expectancy. "But this baby girl, Dan, and all her strange and beautiful little sisters are so alert and engaged already. They self-soothe, they listen so intently when you speak to them. It's as if they know why they're here. Oh God! I sound crazy, don't I? No wonder Claudia insisted I come back to you. I've lost it!"

"You haven't lost a single thing, Nia Bomani!" he scolded. "You don't sound crazy; you sound like a mother." Her passionate eyes softened, and her shoulders curved in around her wild heart. "You've earned the chance to have someone to love and care for in your life, Nia. Hope may come with some unique problems and she may need a little more than the average child to succeed in this life. But who better to champion her than someone like you? You've done the work. Trust yourself."

"I thought I was coming here for permission or a blessing from you," she began, "Or to satisfy Claudia and Ahi. But as usual, you have deferred to me and I see that it was only my own permission I needed to move forward. Even if it's only for a season, I am going to be Hope's mother."

He grinned in tacit agreement, "Congratulations, it's a girl!"

Ahi 2028

United Coalition Great Assembly Hall, Belgium

"Namaste. And thank you Secretary General for that warm introduction. Every time I hear someone presented with the words, 'she needs no introduction' I fear I am in for a repeat performance. And regrettably I do stand before you about to continue a conversation I began with a good number of you years ago. So, for those among our assembly today who may be novice representatives for their territories, I will introduce myself. I am Ahi Mulpuru, PhD. in anthropology and law from Oxford University, way back in the 1980's. A muffled laugh echoed through the chamber. Born in India, but a global citizen, I have spent the last forty years of my career working with the most passionate and intelligent people in the scientific and political worlds to further the chances for peace, health and human rights for all citizens of our planet. As a co-creator of policy to manage our human footprint on our ecosystem, I have lobbied the world's governments, collaborated with experts in many scientific disciplines and personally studied thousands of hours of transcripts and research findings to learn all I could about the changes we've been responsible for making in our planet's health since the dawn of this Anthropocene era."

"All who worked alongside me in these efforts were inspired by the advancement of environmental works to reduce pollution and the many great humanitarian projects fighting human trafficking and abuses against women and children and the aging. And so much has been done to end hunger and bring clean water and medical support to nations previously wanting for these basic human needs. With our efforts concentrated on formatting the progressive goals to which we knew we must aspire we could not have foreseen such a reverse in our momentum as what transpired in the last half a decade, when the tyrant child president of one of the world's greatest nations so crippled his own country that it fell into its second and most vicious civil war, leaving it weak and wounded and easy prey for its enemies. In the wake of this unrest, the underhanded leadership of the Soviets and the North Koreans combined to resurrect the Tsar bombs, 50 mega-ton explosive devises that once deployed, effectively obliterated the islands that were home to the western military installations in the Philippines."

"Now I am schooling you on the obvious. We all watched as the government of our ally was fragmented and ultimately devastated by their own ignorance and apathy. Inevitably, they would succumb to the deceit and trickery of their enemies, bringing down much of the world's financial structure and the international support on which we all depended. So, while this still youthful republic was crumbling, the rest of us have been paying the bills. In this last year since the bombing created the fissure in the ocean floor, catastrophic weather events have increased ten-fold. Ocean levels are rising at an alarming rate, warming some seas, freezing others. Wildlife is disappearing. New opportunistic bacteria and viruses are multiplying by the billions. Crops are failing adding to the ranks of the starving around the globe. Strange mutations in hundreds of infants born to parents in the region of the attacks have become evident. Scientists world-wide have produced data supporting that the fissure on the ocean floor resulting from the bombings is seeping heat and weakening our planet's protections. The Earth sustains our lives largely by retaining the heat in its core with which it was formed. While small amounts of this heat dissipate every day through micro activity this event was not micro but rather mega in nature. This fracture in the deepest layers of terra firma has also made significant changes in the planet's magnetic fields and this can invite the perfect conditions for solar storms and meteor showers, further compromising our safety in orbit."

"We are no longer asking for support and campaigning for unity. We cannot afford such luxury at this stage. We must pool our collective efforts to formulate a plan to mend this tear. Without a consolidated method of protection, our planet faces death. Our planet faces death! Not just the poor people in the undeveloped nations. Not just the blacks. Not just the gays. Not just the women. Not just the people. We will have no planetary home...obliteration! I once feared that our doom would come slowly and under the pressure, we would be driven to eat one another. Hunger, after all, would at least be a basic human need. But with the damage done by this pointless war, I now fear that a cataclysmic event is inevitable if we do not pour our every resource into a plan of reconstruction. If we survive, we may yet have time to recover and reverse the demolition course upon which our habits of disrespect and gluttonous consumption have placed us."

"So I beseech you all, return to your universities and think tanks and scientific associations and create a solution. This is not a time for egos or brute strength, arguing and politics, but rather a time for interdependence and solid problem-solving skills. We are a gifted species. We must not let this temporal event become a fatal one. I am officially moving that the Coalition form a committee to be created within this session of every country's most respected physicists, engineers, designers, architects, and oceanographers. I request a vote of all nations present today, Mr. Secretary."

As Ahi relinquished the podium, a murmur began in the chambers of the great hall. The Secretary General returned to center stage and began the voting process. Ahi, drained, left the chamber and with great effort made her way to Claudia, waiting in the wings. She embraced her wife and leaning on her for support, exited the building toward their idling car. Their driver was quick to his feet and opened the door for the two. Hurrying from the building behind them Barrett Davies caught up just before the car door was closed.

"Ahi, Claudia, wait!" He implored the driver, "Wait, please."

"It's alright, Joffrey." Ahi assured the giant Egyptian.

Claudia objected. "Not tonight, Barrett, she's had enough."

"But Dr. Dereksen, that was so amazing. The world is voting on what Ahi has laid before them."

Taking Claudia's pale hand, Ahi calmed her beloved, "My darling, I'll be fine as soon as we get back to the hotel and get a bite." She offered her own dark hand to Barrett, "Meet us at our suites in about an hour. I still feel like talking." He smiled, kissed her hand and shut the door. He stood a little awestruck as he watched the car disappear down the foggy boulevard. He snapped back to an angry mob marching toward the back door of the hall waving anti-science signs and chanting "Let God work!"

Back at the hotel, Claudia called down for a small spread of cheeses, nuts and fruit. She was pouring the wine when Joffrey dubiously eyeing him, ushered Barrett into the front room of the suites. "I promise not to wear her out tonight, Claudia," he began. "But I feel like I have to capture her emotions right away."

"She had her first chemo round this week. Did you know

this? This is the first day she's remained out of bed for more than a few hours." Claudia filled a plate for Joffrey and signaled the scowling brown man to take it into his room. "Help yourself, Barrett. She'll be out in a minute." She gathered two glasses of wine and retreated with Joffrey to afford the two their privacy.

Barrett broke off a piece of cheese and poured a glass of the dark merlot, refreshed his phone and searched the screen for the recording app. He had time for a couple of almonds and another piece of cheese before his subject emerged from her bedchambers. Standing, he greeted her, "Ahi, thank you so very much for taking this time with me. I know you're tired and Dr. Dereksen told me about the chemo last week. I didn't…"

"Shush, Barrett. I would not do this tonight if I did not feel up to it." Taking a glass in her hand, she gestured to the young journalist to pour.

He obliged and picked up a plate. "Would you like something?"

"No, Son. But help yourself. You are so skinny, Barrett. You must eat more. You remind me of the children in India, too skinny."

He smiled and gratefully indulged his hostess. He had thought himself too excited to eat but the smoky cheeses and hearty wine made his mouth water for more. It had been hours since he last ate, and Ahi always seemed to read him as if she had a sixth sense about these things. "Ok, now tell me what you are feeling at this very moment." he probed. "You've just addressed all the most progressive national leaders of the world about the most ominous circumstances we've ever faced. I can't imagine what is going through your mind right now."

"Honestly?" She sipped at her wine and settled back into the chaise, gathering a pillow from behind her back and propping her elbow upon it. "I'm not sure." Barrett leaned forward in anticipation as she continued. "I am so emotionally tired of pleading for the lives of these foolish people. How much more can one endure?"

"Who exactly do you mean when you say, 'these foolish people'? I mean you bloody well spoke to just about every country on the planet tonight. Which ones are the fools?"

"Hm, good question, Barrett. All of us I guess." She nodded toward the cheese and he cut her a few small pieces and handed her a plate and napkin. "I know we've talked about my father working for Prince Benjamin and The Preservation Foundation. Remember me telling you how he took me to the Sundarbans to tag and track the Bengal Tigers." He nodded. "These animals, Barrett, they were amazing to me, such exquisite beauty and mystery. My father was entranced by them too and swore to protect them from civilization encroaching on their habitat, and pollution and poachers. Poaching, it would seem, was the one thing my father would not tolerate. The senseless killing of these amazing creatures sickened him."

"Yes, Ahi. I remember. You were fourteen, isn't that right?"

"Yes. The year I turned fourteen. The first night we arrived in the park, I saw an adult tiger that had been trapped and killed. The poachers had been frightened off before they could finish skinning the great cat. It was nothing like I had ever seen in my life. This majestic animal lay all but decapitated with his black and orange stripes matted with blood, his hide partially peeled from his powerful musculature. I remember his golden eyes gazing flatly ahead. His mouth had fallen open and his tongue lay limp between his enormous teeth. I was horrified by the sight of it all. But my father's response to this left me absolutely stricken. He fell to his knees next to this lifeless beast and wept. Until that moment, my father was only an idea of a man to me. He stood for things. But these things were concepts, ideals. I was brought up to respect him for his manner of thinking about these things. He was a brilliant biologist who chose to serve the creatures of this Earth with veneration and reverence. This crime had torn at the very fiber of his soul. And in that moment, I saw the kind of man I never knew he was. His devotion to these animals and to his work was more than philosophies to be contemplated and defended. I saw his heart in action. It connected him to me like nothing I had ever experienced with him before."

"Ahi, you didn't tell me any of this when you talked about him before."

"That's because of what happened next."

"What happened?"

"We stayed on in the park for a couple more days. I spent the time shadowing my father wherever he went. I met incredible people all passionate about preserving the tiger population. I felt a part of something truly good and important."

"Of course, how could you feel anything else? What a formative experience."

"Yes. But when we left the park and began our trek home, we were to pick up my father's cousin in the east and so we traveled through the portions of Bangladesh that had become caught up in the Bengali's call for self- determination rights."

"The genocide?"

Ahi winced as a thin pain jettisoned from her armpit to the port in her chest just above her heart. Her physical pain and her visceral memory collided in the moment. "*Searchlight* had begun, and the Butcher of Bengal had started preying on the Bengali's. Muslim religious leaders had declared all Bengali women 'gonimoter maal', public property, spoils of war. We traveled through the streets where we had passed so many times before to enjoy the open markets and cafes. But the sights were much different now. Soldiers with machetes patrolling up and down the walkways. Families being herded like cattle away from their homes. Young girls, not much older than myself, openly beaten by multiple assailants. Their clothes being torn from their trembling bodies while groups of men stood laughing and shouting obscenities at them. Our car stopped to allow a cart to pass and I looked out my window and saw a spectacle I have been unable to escape from for fifty-six years. A young Bengali woman whose hands were tethered above her head to a signpost, her blood-stained legs publicizing her rape, lay with her abdomen ripped open and her organs being torn from their cavities by a pair of dogs." She clenched her mouth and continued, "Vomit rose in my neck and I looked into her face. She had the same dead-eyed stare that I'd seen on the face of the tiger my father wept over on the Bay of Bengal just days before. I reached over the front seat for his shoulder with tears streaming down my cheeks and said 'Father, why?' And his assistant next to me in the back seat grabbed my hand away and pulled me back into my place."

"What did he say?"

"Nothing. Nothing, Barrett. The man who had just days before endeared himself to me for what I thought would be a lifetime, suddenly became complicit in this senseless carnage. How could his culture, our culture, *my* culture be so insanely dichotomous? How could this man weep over the mistreatment of an animal and silently condone the ravaging of this helpless girl? What if this was me? And indeed, Barrett, that girl lying lifeless and so cruelly slaughtered *was* me. She was the child of a mother and a father. She was a sister and a friend. She had a heart and a mind and a unique relationship with the universe. And she was left used and then gutted by savages whose aim was to dehumanize her. But what of their own humanity?"

"They had none, Ahi! Men like that possess no human nature. They themselves are the animals they think they are destroying." He shook his head with shame and indignation. They were both near tears.

She inhaled deliberately and squeezed her eyes tightly to keep from crying. "I won't cry for us. I will not! We have followed the wrong chiefs. We have become a world of self-destructive persons. And now it seems we are alone in the wilderness. Mother Earth has every reason to shake us off once and for all. And if we don't come together now, she will succeed."

"This is the legacy of the '*manthropacene* era', Ahi," Barrett charged. "This dominance of the planet and all who inhabit it, animal or human, that ushered in such devastating wars, pollution, famine, disease and the wasting of all our natural resources. This is what you've been fighting against your whole career – your whole *life*!" His raised voice signaled the two in the other room. "This is what your story will help to explain and expose."

"But who will remain to read it?"

"Dear doyenne, we have to survive this. You and I still have much work to do."

"I am beginning the end of my turn, sweet boy. *You* must do the work for us both. I have said my piece for the last time…again."

"And on that note, I think we'll take our leave, young Mr. Davies," Claudia announced as she swooped back in from the adjoining room, obviously having listened for her cue from behind the door for some time. "You can call again next week when we're back at Oxford, Barrett. But she has to get her rest now. I insist."

Ahi took Claudia's hand and shrugged at the young man. "The boss has spoken. I'd pack it in if I were you, Barrett. She's terrifying." She winked. He rose, humbly bowed to them both and with a hand over his heart, mouthed a silent "thank you" and showed himself out.

Claudia took her partner's glass and returned it to the table. "Come on, *doyenne,* you've had enough saving the world for one night. We all have. Let's get you to bed."

"You know, that kid reminds me of you when we were in

school together. Remember how you hounded me, calling and sending notes?" The two women labored to their feet and facing one another, embraced. "Do you remember how sweet it was when I let my guard down and accepted this? I do, Claudia. I remember it all." Her lover smiled and her pale blue eyes filled with tears. Ahi touched a tender fingertip to Claudia's face to catch the first salty drop that found its way down her powdered cheek.

"I remember you terrorizing that little gypsy girl in senior school," Claudia sniffled.

"Shit! Your memory is so bloody much better than mine! I always start us at University. You hell bent on making the molecules behave and me trying to unwind the mysteries of tyranny," Ahi mused. "Don't start crying now, or we'll never stop."

"I'm sorry, my heart. I feel like the whole world has been after you since we met. And now even though you've tried all your life to save every damnable soul in it, it's coming for you once and for all. I can hear the footsteps of our mortality, Ahi. We are losing our grip on the mortal coil. Can we not lay down our weapons and surrender in these final days? Or must we struggle and fight all the way up to the last minute?"

Abruptly grabbing her wife's arms and giving her a gentle shake, Ahi snapped, "Surrender? And what makes you think these are the final days?" Their eyes locked, both of them seemingly startled at her response then Ahi's expression softened, and a smirk immerged, "Fuck it. Yes! Let's give the whole bloody thing up and go to bed."

"It worked for John and Yoko." Claudia giggled as she took Ahi's elbow and started for the bedroom.

"Do you think we're as good as John and Yoko?" asked Ahi.

"Well I'm as good as John, I don't know about you and Yoko."

"You bitch."

The two made their way to their bed and Claudia helped Ahi out of her robe and slippers and under the covers. "I'll go get your water for your bedtime pills."

"Thank you, Claud. I think I'll need a half a pain pill tonight too, if I'm going to get any rest." Ahi tucked her extra pillows under her knees and removed her eyeglasses then called to her wife, "May I have more wine instead of that water you're going for, darling?"

"Why not?" Claudia called back from beyond the door. "We might as well finish it off."

"Now you're talking," Ahi responded to herself. "What did I do to deserve such a fine woman to love and care for all these years? Thank you, sweet Universe."

Claudia returned with a glass of merlot for each of them, a medicine cup with half a dozen various capsules and tablets, and the remainder of the snacks from Barrett's visit. "He's so sweet and his stuff is brilliant," she stated handing off one glass of the wine and placing the food atop the nightstand within Ahi's reach. "But it's precisely that star-struck fanatic vibe that I assume you're alluding to that reminded you of me, that I'm worried about. He doesn't know when to quit. You are human, you know, Ahi. And right now, you're fragile. He needs to know there are boundaries."

"And what are the consequences for overstepping those boundaries? If he doesn't help me sound the alarm this time, there will be no one left to enforce those boundaries. You know as well as I do that we are the lucky ones. We've lived a good long life with many successes. We *can* lie down. We *can* quit, but what about Barrett and his generation? What about Nia and Hope? He is only just beginning to create his own mythology out of the chaos he was handed in this world. Doesn't his story deserve to be told? Don't the bright ones among the idiots deserve to have a chance at life, at loving, at living?"

"Yes, love. We'll save each other. We must. No one knows better than I how dire it all is, Ahi. We will find a way to keep going." Claudia tucked herself in beside her wife and carefully and tenderly stroked the thin skin covering the port for her chemotherapy. She examined its edges as it rose out of her décolletage like the end of a perfectly broken bone. "Will you promise to do the same? Will you find a way to keep going, darling?"

"And what else would I do?" Ahi answered and gently gripped Claudia's hand then closed her tired eyes.

Happy Birthday!

"Where are they?" Nia playfully bounced Hope in her arms trying to keep the twelve-month-old engaged until their guests arrived in the terminal. "Is that Auntie Claudia? Where is Auntie Ahi?" The baby fidgeted and reached for strangers in the bustling crowd at the airport, smiling openly at everyone whose eye she caught. People delivered their usual soft glances at her round sweet face, followed by their pat shock at the sight of her one crystal-like eye. Nia had gotten so used to these typical responses, that she rarely even noticed any more. She was far too excited about looking out for her friends than what anyone around her was doing. It had been months since she had seen the women in London when she visited with Hope to see Ahi after the surgery. She was delighted that she felt well enough to fly out to celebrate Hope's big day. Spying the two emerging from the tunnel she called, "There they are!" Thrusting her infant daughter's fat little arm above her head, she wagged it mercilessly. "Auntie Claudia! Auntie Ahi!" The baby giggled and squealed as the two lumbered toward them, bags in tow.

"Hope Darling!" Ahi was the first to reach them. "You're so beautiful!" Kissing Nia, Ahi released the handle on her luggage and grabbed the bouncing baby from her arms.

"Oh!" Nia chirped, "Are you sure? She's so heavy, Ahi. Be…"

"You couldn't keep her from this child if you wrestled her to the ground." Claudia explained, "She pushed an old woman back into her seat on the plane because she was taking too long getting her bag from the overhead." She hugged the young mother. "We'll have to walk back home."

They made their way through the busy airport to the car and on to the new flat into which Nia and Hope had moved. Entering with the baby still snug in her arms, Ahi looked the place over. "Well done, you."

Nia smiled, "Do you like it?"

"Very nice, Dr. Bomani," Ahi teased.

"A damn sight better than that hovel you lived in before Hope," Claudia responded setting the bags down. "This is more what you need, love."

"It's a three bedroom and Hope's school is two blocks over on the way to the Institute, even though I'm still taking her into work with me most days."

Dancing Hope around the living room, Ahi sang, "Going to work with Mum is not much fun, I've got a dirty bum, Mum where are the nappies?"

"Oh no, Ahi give her up, I thought I smelled something rancid!" Nia plucked her daughter from her friends embrace and lifted her bottom up to her nose. "Oh yes! That's my daughter. How someone who is such a joy can smell so hideously rotten is beyond me! Come see the nursery you two," she implored.

Claudia collapsed on the sofa and waved Ahi on to watch the show. She eased her head back and closed her eyes while she listened to her family cooing and giggling changing the baby. A slow satisfying smile crept across her tired face and she uttered a quiet, "Thank you, God and all your friends for my girls."

"I can't believe how good she looks," Nia interrupted the prayer on her way to the bin with the diaper. "I thought she'd be tired from the flight, but she is in there sitting crisscross-applesauce on the floor playing puppets!"

"She's done so well with everything."

"You on the other hand, my dearest, look like warm shit." Nia stepped over the luggage and plopped down next to her teacher, friend and Godmother to Hope, threw her arm around her shoulder and asked, "How is she really doing?"

Claudia sighed and gripped Nia's hand. "There were bits they couldn't get with the surgery and haven't responded to the chemo." Nia's head bent into Claudia's. "They want to radiate next. But she wouldn't start until she came for Hope's birthday because she can't be around you two once she begins radiation treatment."

"Claudia, she didn't need to wait."

The middle-aged scientist shook her head, "She wasn't having any of it, child. You know my wife."

Ahi rejoined the two, walking the chubby Hope by the fingers until she reached the couch. "Look at this big girl, Auntie Claud."

"She's a treasure!" Claudia reached for the bubbling babe. "She's our joy."

"So, Nia, we haven't talked about the girls in months." Ahi inquired, "What's happening with the Frigus Filiae?"

"Twelve months of data collected every thirty days has shown no deviations from normal growth activity." Nia reported, "They all still have the pineal over-activity and the subnormal temps, but all are meeting their developmental milestones and thriving."

"And their vision?" Claudia asked while trying to get a closer look at Hope's eyes to see for herself.

"Perfectly normal."

"Amazing." Ahi going for the baby again, "I'm sure Claudia has already spilled my beans?"

"Radiation?"

"Yes. Bloody hell!" Ahi bounced the baby on her knees, playing as she complained, "What the hell else will they have old Ahi do to keep from circling the drain, Hope Darling?"

"When do you get started?"

"As soon as we get back to London town, upside down, my doctor's a clown!"

Sensing the need to change the subject, Nia asked, "And what of The Deep since the elections, Claudia?"

Dr. Dereksen straightened in her seat and started, "Damn these ignorant asses! We've spent the last twenty-one months trying to convince the world leaders what the actual damage really is and now we have a whole new bunch of egomaniacs to educate!" She reddened. "They don't think the damage is that significant! They're arguing that the Weber Deep, as massive as it is, has posed no threat. And, that by insisting on referring to the fissure as *dangerous* and *destructive*, we're creating unnecessary fear with all our 'dooms day predictions'! Those are just the politician's misinformed arguments. That's not even counting the religious groups that are protesting the labs all over the globe because they've been predicting the end of the world for a thousand years and they think we're going to cheat them out of the rapture!"

"It's climate change all over again," Ahi piped in.

"The time we're wasting trying to establish a truth from which to start is infuriating! We've got prototypes of giant magnets ready to assemble and labs set up in five different countries where we are already modeling the experiments, but we can't get the bloody world to agree on what to do next! We can't close the fissure without returning the magnetism of the outer core and we can't create a magnet that will sustain a field long enough to transfer a charge in those temperatures. It's too damn cold!" She checked her rage and added, "I don't see how we can accomplish anything asking for permission. We're never going to get it. We need to go underground."

"You're such an outlaw! We're rallying our forces, Hope Darling. Aunt Claudia and I are going to make the wankers sit up and take notice. Yes we are."

"Sit up wankers! Sit up wankers!" The women chanted and clapped to Hope's delight. A sweet delirium set into their tired spirits and they all fell out laughing and loving on the sweet baby.

~

Nia rose the next morning to find Claudia already up and making the tea. The two kissed and whispered quiet good mornings to keep from waking Hope and Ahi. They read the news on their tablets sitting silently across from one another at the breakfast table when the front door slowly opened, and Ahi appeared with Hope in the pram.

"Look who's up, Hope Darling!" Ahi beamed.

"What the bloody hell, Ahi?" Claudia started while Nia sat frozen and slack-jawed, "Where the hell have you two been?"

"We left a note. Didn't you see it?" The women shook their heads. "We've been to the corner for a biscuit and tea, just the two of us."

"How? I didn't hear a thing. I'm usually such a light sleeper." Nia felt a wave of nausea as she realized that someone woke her infant daughter, changed and dressed her, and left the flat with her without waking her mother. "Was she good for you, Ahi? Did she behave?"

Sensing her unease, Ahi immediately took the baby from her belts and delivered her into her mother's arms. "She was so good, Mum. And she only had one little biscuit. I took the bottle you made for her last night and figured we'd have a proper breakfast when we got back. You and Claudia were still sleeping. And we wanted to go where we could talk."

"It's all good, Auntie." Nia sighed and checked her paranoia so as not to embarrass the already shamed Ahi.

"You'd have given her a heart attack if she'd have checked

on this little girl and found a damn note, Ahi," Claudia scolded.

"No, no it's fine, girls." Nia reassured. "This is good for us. She needs to be out with other people besides me. I'm smothering her." The words came out just ahead of a wall of tears. The older women flocked to their young ward.

"What is it?" Claudia probed.

"I'm sorry, I'm a mess. I wanted this to be a happy occasion and I'm so filled with worry for Ahi and every day I wonder if I'm doing this right and what's going to happen and how long will we all have each other?"

"Nia, Nia," Ahi began as she knelt down next to the sobbing mother. "Shhh. Nia, you are just feeling overwhelmed. You've taken on the life of another. You're somebody's mother now."

"Ahi's right, Nia," Claudia chimed in. "You're doing fine. This baby is well and happy." Nia nodded, wiping her face and smiling down at her beautiful girl. "And you've been overseeing the lives of children you didn't even know for a decade at the Institute. You were made for this."

"That's different, Claud. Those kids' lives were ultimately someone else's responsibility. I just studied them. There's so much more to it. It's every day and all day and all night and in your sleep and I go to work with food on my clothes and I have a twenty-five-pound diaper bag that could double as a survival kit but I consistently forget to pack Maurice the Pig! And I'm exhausted from staying up all night watching her sleep!" The threesome cracked up at the last item in Nia's rant.

"Wait," began Claudia again, "The baby sleeps through the night but you don't?"

"She has slept through the night since I brought her home. She is the most peaceful human I've ever been around. But I can't stop staring at her all night. Not alarmed for her safety or watching to see if she's breathing. I am just mesmerized by her."

Ahi pressed a plump hand of the cherub to her lips and with a gentle kiss whispered, "She's enchanting."

"Truly, it's like she has me in a trance. I'm so in love with her. Is that normal?"

"Let's hope so! What parent doesn't love their child like that?" Claudia wondered aloud. Ahi and Nia both looked at their friend with a darkness that Claudia was too fortunate to understand. They had both been subject to the worst of parental nature. Claudia knew instantly that her comment, though innocent and free from malice had struck a chord she was unable to discern. Embarrassed by her privilege, she fumbled, "Right, yes, well. See, you're a damn site better than a lot of mums and dads then, aren't you?"

“We are doing well, aren’t we Hope?” Nia questioned. “Your momma isn’t a total hack, now is she?”

The baby looked up at the tear-streaked face of her mother, smiled and lulled, “Mummm.”

“And now we’ve heard from the only one who really matters!” Claudia announced. “Let’s get some breakfast in us and get this day started. We came for this child’s birthday celebration!”

“Yes, right. Well today we have infant massage at Susan’s. Ahi, I thought you might want to take part in that.”

“Please and thank you. Sounds delightful.”

“And I thought I could take Claudia to the clinic and show her a few things and then we’ll all meet up for group at the Institute.”

The women agreed on the schedule and set out to accomplish their tasks.

~

The clinic was bustling with interns and specialists. The Frigus Filiae had made it to their one-year milestone and the volume of data being collected and analyzed was staggering. Claudia and Nia downloaded data from the charts for rounds and began discussing the exams that Hope had already undertaken at this mark and the rest of the girls would systematically be subjected to: MRI and CT scans of their brains, full body PET scans, cognitive tests, sensory measurements including visual acuity, hearing screenings, and tactile stimulation examinations. Every discipline of the institute was engaged in the assessments of these toddlers. The fact that they'd made it a year and not lost a single baby to illness or injury or worse was celebrated among Nia's team. But the fact that these children weren't just surviving but thriving meant that not only their care had been exceptional but that the kids themselves were a hearty lot. The two doctors progressed through the busy halls of the hospital and into an observation room connected to the dayroom via a two-way mirror. In the room where the children were engaged in structured play, one by one the baby girls turned from their occupational therapists and looked straight into the mirror as if making direct eye contact first with Nia then with Claudia. Claudia was unnerved but said nothing. Nia met each girl's glance with a thoughtful nod and then gestured to her mentor to do the same. Claudia did as much then said, "That was creepy. Is this a window or a mirror?"

"A mirror." Nia answered.

"Does that happen every time anyone enters the room?"

"Until today, it was just me. I'm anxious to see what the notes from this session look like. I can access them from my computer at home tonight. What are your first impressions?"

"You're right, they look good on paper. Great vitals with

the exception of their temps but if the scans and labs come back within normal limits, they are normal in every other physiological way," Claudia concluded.

"But?"

"But what are socio-cognitive exams displaying? More behavior like what we just saw?" she asked.

"Yes," Nia began. "It's sometimes very subtle but there is an air to these girls."

"They are acutely aware of their surroundings, that's obvious. But what is this quietness? It's almost an eerie peace I sense about them."

"This is what is being reported by speech pathology, occupational therapy, and the psychologists." Nia opened a few charts to compare. "They're using words like 'stoic', 'thoughtful', 'serene', 'Zen-like'. I don't want to make a big deal about it because I think it enhances the weird factor these poor kids have to combat every day but it's definitely something."

"It's something alright." Claudia was only half listening as she became immersed in the charts of first one girl then another. When the current session in the day room ended and the babies were ushered on to the next testing procedure, the room was empty for a moment and then filled again with another group to be examined. Deep in concentration on the material she was reading, it took a nudge from Nia to get Claudia to look up and take note of the magical eyes trained on the two of them. Another crop of toddlers stopped in their tracks until both women met each of their gazes. And then as if flipping a switch, returning their attention to their therapists and resuming the activity at hand. Claudia and Nia slowly turned toward one another, awestruck.

Ahi followed the short stream of parents and babies into the modest home of the infant massage instructor. Hope, a return customer was welcomed back, and Ahi was quietly introduced around. In a large parlor in the front of the house, the dyads took their places on rectangular cushions in a semi-circle on the floor; moms on one end and babies laid out on the remaining length of the pillows. Ahi followed suit and sat cross-legged with the deliciously chunky legs of her charge resting on her silk pants, taking note that at least at first glance, she had the only "atypical" child in the group. The class began with the adults asking the babies for permission to begin, a mark of respect, and then watching for cues of engagement.

While the other grownups struggled to discern their baby's nonverbal signals, Ahi read a resounding "yes" in Hope's centered gaze. The instructor noted the connection from across the room and gave Ahi a wink and a thumbs-up. The class progressed and before long it was obvious that the other kids weren't nearly as engaged as Hope. Two fussed and squirmed off their pillows. One cranked up and flat out cried, causing another two to respond in kind. And the only other tot that stayed still throughout the entirety of the class was a round boy whose mother sighed that she never makes it past the leg routine before he falls asleep, "Just like his father," she complained.

Ahi got the distinct sense that not only did Hope enjoy the tactile sensations of the massage strokes and calming effects of the gentle conversation but that she understood the communication that was taking place between them on a deeper level. Ahi was a champion to all humanity and Hope seemed almost to acknowledge this with reverent notice. The two were lost in each other for the hour when the instructor interrupted their concentration to conclude the session and thank them for their participation. As the others robotically went for their diaper bags and car seats, Ahi stared down at the peaceful Hope and knew she was destined for bigger things. "There are many paths ahead of you, darling girl. But you can choose which way you go with confidence that all are meant for you." The smiling cherub looked intently into the warm eyes of her admirer as if she too knew about the paths and the bigger things.

When Nia and Claudia arrived at the Institute for the group therapy session, they found Ahi and Hope already comfortable with the other parents. They filed in behind the two and waited for the facilitator to begin the session. As with any parents group, there was talk of the basics, teething and feeding and crawling and beginning to walk, but within this group and indeed every one of the gatherings of the parents of these children, there was no talk of anxiety over their development, no sleeping issues, and no crying jags. Instead they talked about their daughters' ability to self soothe and even comfort *them* with their calming energy. The consistency of reports like this among the parents of the girls was as interesting to the researchers as their ability to thrive with their cold body temperatures. With their pineal glands lighting up like Christmas trees on the scans of their brains, the sleep regulation wasn't too big a mystery. Melatonin produced by the pineal gland was a hormone essential for achieving healthy sleep/wake cycles. But the emotional regulation was notable. Most of the children were benefitting from the infant massage classes and most of the parents were comforted by inclusion in them as well as the group therapy opportunities. But this was more than just having support and new skills to bond with their baby girls. These infants were markedly different from their peers. Reflecting these findings, the objective data gathered by the department of psychology was integrated into the physiological examinations and the developmental progress of the girls and a profile was immerging of an emotional hyperawareness that they all seemed to possess. These babies drew people to them. As her mother, Nia felt that draw in her heart from Hope. Professionally though, she and her colleagues alike experienced the same pull from all the Cold Daughters. Even with her feelings of commitment to her daughter aside, Nia knew this was the most interesting work she would ever do.

At the end of the day back at the flat, Ahi fed the baby while Claudia and Nia put the party together. Nia cleared the dinner dishes from the table and finished icing the cake. Claudia blew up balloons and strung streamers from the lights. Hope watched the women working and talking with delight. They lit the single candle and sang to the clapping toddler and cheered when the candle went out and she dug her tiny hands into her cake. The palpable gratitude for the opportunity for them to be together despite the year's challenges gave way to happy tears and hugs and kisses all around. With so much to be thankful for and so much more to navigate in the coming months and years, they indeed had Hope. And that would be their salvation.

Barrett and Ahi 2032

"Another prototype down the pipes." Claudia read the text aloud at Ahi's insistence.

"What was it this time?"

"The land-based models are completely ineffective; the saltwater and currents wreak havoc with the waves created by that kind of electromagnet. And the underwater prototypes need metal compounds that stay magnetized in the cold sea water. There's a very short list of metals that will keep a magnetic charge at those depths and they keep mixing them instead of using pure ores. We've wasted so much of what we have by compounding with everything under the sun to try and create a magnet that's strong enough and will work for long enough to reconstruct the field. And of course, every country that has the ores to mine is leveraging its resources for money or military support or some other form of extortion!" Her wife watched as her blood pressure rose. "This is what has the teams in several regions talking about going covert." Ahi winced with pain and interrupted her wife's train of thought. "I'm sorry, Ahi, damn it! I said no work in this place and I meant it."

"I'm fine. And anyway, I asked, didn't I?"

"Enough talk. You need to rest."

"Barrett's coming in again today, you know."

"Yes. I know. And you know I'm not happy about it."

"I already feel tons better since they sliced that last piece off me and I'll be bored out of my head alone in the apartment. I have to have something to keep myself busy."

"Mmmm. I don't have time to stand here and argue with you. Don't wear yourself out!" Claudia barked, bent to kiss her wife on the forehead and left for the lab.

It had been five years since the diagnosis and there hadn't been a stretch longer than a few months where Ahi wasn't receiving some kind of treatment to fight the cancer. After trials with different chemo drugs, multiple rounds of radiation, and major surgeries, she now had metastatic disease in her bones. The tumors in the bone were responding to treatment though and she was hopeful that if it didn't show up somewhere else, she'd have it licked. Ahi was hopeful. Claudia, ever the skeptic, was less so. They both braved the journey like champions, each crying in the shower to hide their fear and doubt from the other. They had conquered so much as a couple, this would be no different.

In their college years they had come out to their families. Ahi, coming from a traditional Hindu background, argued to her parents that the ancient texts were lacking a straightforward condemnation of the practice of homosexuality, but her mother and father rejected her union with Claudia on the grounds that it didn't align with the sanctity of the traditional family that centered around marriage and children. She was able to remain secretly connected to her younger sister, Padma until their mother's death, but when Ahi tried to come to the funeral, Padma forbade her. She was unable to go against their father's wishes and remain in his good graces, a choice that would forfeit her relationship with Ahi forever. Sri Mulpuru died six months after his wife and Padma died of the same breast cancer that was killing her sister three years after him. Ahi lived with little regret but not having reconciled with her family before they were gone remained a source of quiet shame. She used it to fuel her desire to embrace mankind as her family and serve them even though they did not always want or deserve her efforts. There were hurdles in her professional life as well. Claudia worked among higher thinkers and was seldom made to feel like an outcast and furthermore she didn't care. But Ahi chose a path strewn with small minds and manipulators. She fought for their respect as a woman but doubly so as a lesbian. She didn't advertise her sexuality, nor did she attempt to hide it. She had sought an authentic life since her twenties even though living it sometimes meant painful loss and exclusion. She and Claud had a diverse cluster of devoted friends and colleagues whose support they had counted on heavily over the duration of their union and never more so than since the onset of her illness. With all this love, how could they help but prevail?

She had fallen asleep in the chaise when Barrett buzzed from the street to come up just before ten. She carefully made her way to the door as she was still weak and at risk for falling if she wasn't methodical in her movements. She was settling back down in her coveted spot when Barrett entered the apartment eager to begin their session. He had brought bits of the film for her to preview and was trying not to show how proud he was of the production so far. "I have a surprise for you, Dr. Ahi Mulpuru, World Champion of the Human Race!" he started.

"Is that so, young man?"

"Yes, ma'am, I have a bit of the first couple of montages that we're stringing together. I think it's turning out beautifully."

"Oh yes, let's see." Barrett laid his tablet flat on the coffee table and tapped into the app on his phone to raise the hologram to where Ahi could watch. As the snippets of her career played one after the other, she remembered out loud the times and people in the scenes. "Oh my God, look how young I was, that's when Al first made his documentary. He was so charismatic. Oh, and there I am working on the water project in my home country with Gary and Matt."

"Were you ever star struck, Ahi?"

"No…um…well, no. Not star struck. But I fell totally in love with Matthew. His heart and soul are even more amazing than his talent."

"And his looks?"

"Even though he's not my type, I must admit, he was hot!" The two laughed out loud at this revelation. "Oh my God, what good things these people did and are still doing!"

"These people, and you," Barrett corrected.

"Yes, yes. I made room on the platform and enabled the others to be heard and seen by more who could help the causes along. I know, Barrett. I know I have been blessed to be a kind of an agent of these movements." The two continued watching; she the film and he her reaction to it. "Bradley, what he was able to do to fight against the human traffickers. Saints, these people, Barrett. No less than saintly actions undertaken by all these groups and their volunteers. You know, even the Christians."

"Ha! Ahi, really?"

"Hear me out. You know how I rail against the God-fearing evangelical machine to this day, but there have been so many good, God-*loving* men and women who accomplished so very much in the name of Christ for the good of humanity. Jesus would be overcome with the love these followers have exhibited."

"But…?"

"No buts, Barrett. There have been myriad Christian

charities who truly served humanity over the years. It's just such a shame that there have also been those who misled countless souls in Jesus' name, excluding, judging, and harming those who weren't like them. This isn't news to you. You've known all along how I felt about organized religions. And the Christians aren't the only ones. These systems to which we all subscribe, have good and bad inherent along their continuums. To ignore the worst of the group is no more or less irresponsible than never celebrating the best. The ones who stand out in my experience are the ones who operated alone or with a small group of diverse people and took the world by storm, truly changing something wrong into something beautiful. If you only watch the tear drop into the ocean, it is easy to say no *one* person can make a difference. But, Barrett, if you look at the ripples each tear creates when it drops, you see how far reaching our love can truly become."

His voice to text recorder had caught her quote and he tapped to highlight it for later when she snorted at the next frames. Her being escorted past violent protestors and next being spit on and then another of her being led away in handcuffs. "What do these scenes evoke, Ahi?"

"I can only laugh at them now, Barrett," she began. "I'd be lying if I said I wasn't afraid. Fanatics can be terrifying. It's even more harrowing when the fanatics are in charge! I was less afraid in the mobs calling for my head then I was when I was being arrested in some of these clips. I had death threats and even attempts on my life."

"I remember reading about that in school. They called you the Lorax."

Caught off guard by her own laughter, Ahi grabbed at her ribs in pain.

"Oh no, are you alright?"

"Oh hell, Barrett. I'd forgotten about all that. Yes. 'Death to the Lorax', the signs read. They had a field day with that."

"Now you find it funny?"

"Not funny, as much as laughable, son." She contemplated those moments and reframed her reaction. "I have outlived the threat of their ignorance, those people whose dependence on working for petroleum or coal production, the ones who stood to gain ground if women or girls were kept out of schools or sold for a profit. I told myself at every turn, just stay alive. As long as you are still telling the truth, there's a chance to erase this ignorance. As long as you still stand, you can change hearts and minds. These people, these Lorax haters, they are just like us. Just like you and me with one main difference; the total truth."

"Can you expand on that idea, Ahi?"

"There are facts. Yes?" Barrett nodded. "Claudia and Nia spend their lives calculating the facts, hard evidence about everything in our world. Anything that can be measured or counted or observed and recorded can afford us the facts on any subject. But every human has a narrative built not on facts but on perception. The way in which the facts they become aware of fit into this perception of life becomes their individual truth." She adjusted in her chair for the rest of her rant and Barrett paused the video. "Now many assume that truth and fact are absolutes. But they are not. Facts that can be challenged and stand up to the scrutiny of proof are about as absolute as we can get. But these facts, when seen through the filter of our individual perceptions, can morph and change to benefit our own narrative, to illustrate our own stories, to become our truths. What dictates those narratives?" she asked, rhetorically. "Our cultural tapestries with all the color and texture of the history of our people creating expectations and standards by which we live. This can come from our nationalities, our languages, our faith, our families and our geography. It can also come from the myths we've bought into. And there are so very many human myths. Our faith systems are wrought with them. Our relationships with our deities and our trust in the word of our spiritual leaders as well as the influential people in our everyday lives; our political leaders, professors, our parents, grandparents, siblings, friends and colleagues, all the girls in our group."

"People are probably not even aware of the filters they are absorbing the facts through, are they?"

"It can be so pervasive that it seeps into our pores as children and we can't discern it. It takes a concentrated internal effort to even identify what our truths are, let alone try to understand where they came from and if we even truly subscribe to them ourselves." She shrugged. "Most people don't have the emotional energy or freedom to explore within. And if they do, there are plenty of big systems ready to shut them down and keep them from pondering such things."

"It's what entrapped us all in these cycles of co-dependence."

"We're not trapped, Barrett!" Ahi scolded. "Say it, 'I am not trapped, I am free to pursue my own head and heart in this life. I am not trapped.' Say it, Barrett!"

"I am not trapped. I am…" he stammered.

"Free…"

"Free to pursue my own head in this…"

"And heart!"

"I am free to pursue my own head and heart in this life. I am not trapped."

"Very good." She squirmed in the chaise again to get comfortable and nodded toward the screen to signal Barrett to resume the video. He did so and she again became transported to the times and events displayed.

"Remember this, Ahi?" Barrett paused on a clip of his subject receiving the Nobel Peace Prize for her work in the restoration of the palm oil fields in the rain forests.

"God yes! I was so humbled. I was that tear in the ocean in the fight against deforestation but there I was up there getting dubbed the savior of the Sumatran Orangutan."

"So, is this a positive memory or no?"

"I have to say yes. Any time someone raises the awareness of even one other soul to the plight of something they knew nothing about, it is reason for celebration. I just never felt comfortable taking credit for the whole thing. I've done nothing on my own. As a matter of fact, the only thing I've ever done alone was make mistakes. I've always contended that the only thing we can ever take sole credit for in this life is our blunders."

"But you are an accomplished speaker and activist and author," he touted.

"Law school, volunteers, the best editor and publisher in the business. I've done none of those things without lots of help, son."

"So, what are some of the 'blunders' did you call them, that you *were* solely responsible for?" he probed.

"Ohhh, now we're talking expose`! I'm not so sure your audience is ready for all this then." They laughed at this and so much more between them since their interviews began. A definitive chemistry underlined every exchange. She shared everything and he chose what to include with respect and admiration and never a hint of sensationalism or gratuitous exposure. These two people from such separate generations, ethnicities, and cultures were the very model of cooperation and understanding they both sought to illuminate with this documentary. The two unlikely friends talked and laughed into the evening hours as Ahi told tale after tale of her miss steps and embarrassments including everything from bungled political coups to pantyhose mishaps on the world stage. The evening eased into the comfort of a favorite old sweater and time got lost in the pockets. They both jumped with surprise when Claudia bustled through the front door of the apartment with Joffrey lugging groceries in tow behind her.

"Oh my God!" Claudia erupted. "Don't tell me you've been here, grilling her all day Barrett Davies." Ahi and Barrett were struck still by the sudden burst. Claudia muscled her satchel and bags into the already full arms of their loyal valet and pushed him into the kitchen. Returning she kicked up again, "I swear to God I will crush you like a grape if you've made her sick with all this activity."

"Claudia, darling…" Ahi attempted to soothe as Barrett

closed down his devices and prepared for a hasty exit.

"Don't darling me, Dr. Mulpuru! You know better." Barrett was on his feet by this time and bowed his head in shame. "What have you two got to say for yourselves?"

"Sorry, Dr. Dereksen, we really didn't overdo it. Did we, Ahi?"

"No, Barrett. Claudia, we were having a ball. We just lost track of time. I haven't moved from this spot. I'm perfectly comfortable. And we've been talking and laughing. Show her the snippets, son."

"Not right now, Barrett. Have you eaten? Have you stretched or walked even a little?" The angry scientist stared at the two waiting for an answer. "She can't just sit for hours, Barrett. She has to move and stretch and eat and hydrate or she will weaken and dehydrate and develop blood clots in her legs that could travel to her heart or lungs or brain and kill her. Are you aware of all this, *son*?"

"No, ma'am."

"No. But you are." She turned to focus her attention on her wife. "Are you trying to kill yourself? Is this some exercise in self-destruction?"

"Barrett, I think you'd better leave before my wife loses

any more of her shit. Thank you for coming by, I had a lovely time. I'll call you next week and set up a time when we can meet in my office. I'm sure I'll feel like getting out of here by then." The young reporter slipped awkwardly by a steaming Claudia and out the door. "Smash him like a grape? What the hell was all that then, Claud? This isn't about Barrett."

Without another word, Claudia turned on her heel and stomped out of the room onto the terrace and slammed the door. She looked out over the gardens of the flats on Holywell Street and beyond at the glow of the lights from the university. They had haunted these streets and boroughs for nearly sixty years since the time she joined her lover at college. She thought about the first nights she spent in the dorms and cheap apartments she and Ahi occupied "as friends" until they came out. She remembered holding her sobbing partner when her father had called her a disgrace to the family and ordered her to leave his house and never return. Claudia had cradled her and willed her own strength to hold out for them both while they recovered from the lashing. Then with every choice of her life, she had tried to create a loving and safe environment for the woman she loved. And here they were at the end of their lives together and she was losing control of that safety net. She could no longer keep her precious love from the grips of her disease or the uncertainty of the world events that threatened them both, and indeed everything around them. It was all becoming too much to hold at bay. She was feeling her courage wane and along with it the strength to keep up the brave front she had practiced since she committed to Ahi so long ago.

Ahi tip-toed into the kitchen and carefully helped Joffrey heat some soup and toss a simple salad. He insisted on helping her to the table and he finished the meal and was setting the places when Claudia returned composed. “Something smells delicious.”

“Are you alright?” her wife asked.

“I’m sorry, my dears. I am just so frustrated with the lack of progress and support at the lab. Politics and special interests, these idiots have no idea what we’re up against.”

“You’re going to solve the problem, Claudia. You have to,” Ahi declared.

“Someone has to.” She said it with ebbing hope. She said it and felt her skeleton soften and bow from the weight of it. She said it and heard herself saying it but attached no expectation to it. Someone did indeed have to solve the problem, or no one would remain to solve another. But the burden of it was starting to become heavier with the threat of everything close to her fading away. “I’m sorry for lashing out at you and poor Barrett. I am ashamed of how I spoke to you both. I’m nobody’s mother. I’ll call him and apologize after dinner.” Ahi placed a forgiving hand on Claudia’s and the three shared a quiet dinner.

"I understand completely…no, thank you. Yes goodnight." Barrett tapped his earpiece off and breathed easier. He knew he would have to walk the line where Claudia was concerned if he was going to be able to finish the project with Ahi. And not only was time running out for good days with his subject, but the hourglass was emptying on humanity. And he could only imagine what Claudia and the other scientists and designers, and engineers were up against. He lay on his bed in his modest loft and felt small. His project had had such heft to it when he started and when Ahi fell ill, it took on a new sense of urgency that caused him to become quite single minded in his efforts to tell her story.

He had followed her career as a first-year law student and then after a crisis of conscience, changed tracts in school to pursue a career in documentary filmmaking. He was no longer intrigued by the ability to bend the truth to fit the law, now he was on a mission to expose the truth to challenge the law. The time he spent with Ahi poring over transcripts of the most important changes in policy and world edicts ever penned, was better than the finest education offered at any institution of higher learning. The anecdotes she recalled about the people and events that shaped her career were nothing short of fascinating. She was a talented communicator and a gifted storyteller. Her warmth made him heartsick for his own family. He turned onto his side and focused on a framed photo of his mother and father taken just before he left Kilkenny for university. His dad with his handlebar mustache and his mom's smiling eyes stared back at their boy from the picture. They'd been confused and a little disappointed by his change of careers but had supported his decision and shared in his enthusiasm for the project with Ahi. They were very progressive thinkers themselves and appreciated his interest in someone they held in such high regard.

"I'll take better care of her going forward, Ma. I'll be mindful and trust that she always works too hard and I should be more aware of her frailty." A lonely tear wound its way around the frame of his glasses to his pillow as he promised his parents he'd make them proud and then gave into sleep.

Nia and Hope 2032

"Two more lines, Hope. Then you can quit for the night." Nia and her kindergartner were practicing their handwriting.

"I like this letter, Momma." Hope's tongue traced the movement of her pencil as she repeated the capital *G* for two more lines.

"When you're done, we can pick out a story for bed. Sound good?" The intent child nodded as she continued with her task. Nia tidied the kitchen and started the dishwasher then darted into the bedroom for pajamas and back to the bathroom to fill the tub. Their routine was familiar but flexible. Play after school, then dinner, then homework, then bath and bed. Nia's compulsion for order was hard to relax to accommodate the unpredictable turns in a day with a five-year-old. But she'd been able to curb her anxiety over it considerably. And Hope had no idea how maddening it was for her mother to be even slightly off schedule. That was the true test of how well Nia had adjusted. Keeping Hope's life as carefree as possible was Nia's mission. She had no idea what was in store for her unique daughter and she was not about to cause her any undue angst with her own rigid tendencies.

The writing pages were retired to the backpack and the pair skipped into the bathroom where bubbles and songs commenced. Wrapped in a warm towel, Hope dripped on the mat while dressing, stood on tiptoe for teeth and hair brushing and then finally settled into the best spot in the house for story time. Her bed was the stuff of dreams, layered with soft quilts and pillows, Maurice the Pig held in a headlock by the yawning girl, and multicolored twinkle lights strewn between the bedposts. And again, for what seemed like the one-millionth time, they read

The Giving Tree.

Hope cackled and squirmed as her mother turned the pages of her favorite book and when they were done, looked directly into Nia's loving eyes and asked, "Why don't I look like you, Momma?"

Nia tried not to look terrified. She had known this question would come and she'd practiced her answer over and over in her mind. But somehow, now she couldn't recall a shred of what she'd rehearsed. "Well, Baby," she began. "You were given to me by another momma and daddy."

"Who's momma and daddy?"

"Well…um…yours, my sweet."

"But *you're* my momma."

"Yes, love, I am your momma and I love you to the moon!" Nia reached in for a tickle to give herself more time. "I was alone, just working in the clinic with no one to love."

"And you wished for me."

"And I wished for a baby girl to call my own. I wished and wished for you. And one day a momma and daddy came into the clinic and had you. And even though they loved you very much, they couldn't take care of you."

"So, you did?"

"So, I asked them if I could please help because I wanted you so very much and they said I could have you but only if I promised to love you as much as they did." The charming Hope stared wide-eyed at Nia's flushing face. "And I said, I promise to love her as much as you do and more and more always and all ways."

"And they said, ok?"

"They said, 'You're the one. You're Hope's Momma!' And I was so excited! I brought you home and fed you and changed your poopy nappies and we danced and cuddled and read stories."

"And you kept your promise huh, Momma?"

"I love you more and more always and all ways."

Hope hugged Nia's neck and kept on, "Do *you* have a momma."

"Oh yes, my love, everyone has a momma, but we'll talk about my momma another night. You need to get to sleep. Remember we're going on our hike tomorrow morning with Beth and her family." Nia tucked her daughter in.

"Four corners?" Hope requested. Nia kissed her chin, both cheeks, and forehead.

"Mwah kiss," prompted the girl.

"Mwwwwaaaaaaaahhh!" With the final love for the day planted on her daughter's rosebud lips and the lights off, Nia pulled the door closed and breathed a sigh of relief. What just happened? How had she done? She ambled to the fridge and reached for a beer. Had she answered the question? Was it ok to put her off about her own family? Yes. It was too much for a five-year-old at bedtime for God's sake. She had told her she was adopted. She had had the talk and it went well. But was it too soon? Should she have put her off about that too? No. She asked and Nia answered. That's how it was supposed to go. Hope would absorb what she could about it and if she had other questions later, Nia would answer those too. But she'd have to be much older to hear about Nia's parents. That tale was just not suitable for the very young. But she'd done ok. She tipped the beer and closed her eyes as the bitter cold malt filled her throat. "Holy Mary, Mother of God!" she swore to herself. She grabbed another beer and took the bottles into the living room where she methodically assembled the backpacks for their hike the next day. Grateful to have a mindless task to accomplish, she drifted in and out of a haze until it was complete then she finished her first beer and changed into her bedclothes. Propped up in bed, she popped the top on the next one and tapped her tablet to review the files from the latest department summaries on the Frigus Filiae.

Speech Pathology:

All subjects in clinical study group are displaying typical individual speech and swallowing patterns and normal range of abilities. All testing results are within normal limits. The only deviation from baseline was observed when the test subjects were observed together, less verbal communication was required between them to achieve the same results as compared to the typical subjects in the control group. Objectively, they appear to have an unspoken understanding of one another.

Psychology:

General results of clinical examination for individual cognition and emotional response within normal limits with one exception; of note to the psychology staff is the absence of any aggressive or competitive behavior as compared to control. Example: Subjects Gemi and Beatriz were observed in the cartoon exercises known to incite aggressive or defensive behavior in typical subjects of comparable age and development. Both females showed measured restraint in their reactions. Staff recording "peaceful" reactions with "gratitude" and "forgiveness" marked in their responses. This result was mirrored by all the test subjects in stark contrast to those in the control group.

Occupational Therapy:

This study group is mostly unremarkable when compared to control. Physical and cognitive responses to test challenges are within normal limits with no deviation in normal behavior with the exceptions that timed tasks were completed in less than the allotted period without reported or observed anxiety typical in control subjects. Also, test group subjects working in clusters to complete examinations were markedly cooperative and displayed democratic collaboration and team-building skills atypical of children of this chronologic age.

Diagnostic Imaging:

Test subjects continue to display overactive pineal glands under magnetic resonance imaging. Waking study results conclude 74% more recordable activity than control group. Sleeping evaluations revealed 98% greater activity than typical subjects. No evidence of neoplasms or other deviations by PET scan. Hemodynamics remain supportive for normal circulation and oxygen delivery despite the temperature abnormality present since birth.

Family Psychology:

Recordable data of family units observed appear to be stable overall. The units studied at this time stamp have exhibited model communication, no apparent anxiety producing behavior and a calm group dynamic. Both adoptive and natural parent sets are reporting positive sleep/wake cycles, task completion, and family interaction. Siblings of the test subjects are notably more relaxed and less antagonistic, displaying objective resolution of rivalry and competition. A pattern of creative play is on the rise in spontaneous activity across the board with every test subject's family. Example; comparing the families of Azriella, Rima, and

Lucy, this staff observed when given the chance to watch the television, play a board game or cook a healthy snack together, all three families chose to make the snack. Each group created a different dish without recipes, every individual family member contributing something unique that complimented the dish. This example was born out repeatedly when creative choices were offered.

The summaries had been steadily developing these same patterns since the research began. All the girls and those in their close proximity displayed these Zen-like qualities when faced with communicating, problem solving or conflict resolution. Nia had insisted on using the girls' names instead of anonymous markers for the first time in her career. She had anticipated push-back from the board of directors on this but had gotten none. She was sure that she'd have to defend herself as Hope's mother and the head of the research, but the board seemed to recognize the importance of the personalizing of these subjects. The girls had overcome the local stigma that arose around their abnormalities and had earned the respect of the institute's benefactors.

As always, she read the reports with one eye on the research and the other on Hope. For now, the status quo was enough to keep them safely moving forward. Data would continue to be collected as long as the funding kept coming, and that seemed likely to be well into the girls' adolescence. Nia swallowed her last swig of beer and settled back into bed.

She'd had the talk and it went well.

Quantum Biology 2037

Claudia sprawled across one end of the sofa in her office at the lab, where she had woken from a power nap minutes before a group from her team poured in discussing the most recent project failure. She was spending more and more time in the lab and asking the same of her crew. The cluster of designers and physicists presented with a communal fatigue that Claudia felt both proud of and guilty for simultaneously. The discussion volleyed back and forth among the team members about the latest attempt to recreate the earth's magnetic field using a submerged magnet, as Claudia listened.

"Dr. Dereksen, we think we've narrowed the metals down to iron manganese, nickel oxide, chromium, or hematite. And this time we discovered that the centrifugal force was not calibrated to the proper speed to achieve a sustainable field with any of them. So while the spin cycle can be adjusted, we still don't know how to create an apparatus that can continue to spin indefinitely."

"You make it sound like a washing machine! If they would only listen when we say that the field is only half the problem!"

"Right, we don't have to engage it indefinitely, just long enough to recharge the core."

"But then we have to close the fissure somehow to keep the current circulating or its all for naught."

"People, people, please! We were all taught to look beyond these questions, to create something original. But that is impossible. Every idea we seek is already out there, we just have to tune in to what we know and more importantly what we *need*. Or rather, what Mother Earth needs." Claudia sat more erect to enter the debate. “This is why each and every one of you is part of this unit. We know how to build a gigantic magnet. The saltwater and cold depths have been a challenge. The amount and availability of the ores is presenting a minor problem. And you’re wasting your time with those alloys. We should only be focusing on pure metal ores! If solving one piece of this puzzle creates a Band-Aid for the issue, then we have got to apply the Band-Aid! Creating the magnet will get us halfway and protect us from,” she paused to grimace, “inclement weather.”

“I heard that Stanof’s predictions are honing the dates and times down to within weeks and even days of a catastrophic solar event,” offered one of the team.

“I read that it’s going to be the winter of 2040, around the solstice,” confirmed another.

“The Bodhi Bahrat says, ‘the sun will stand still on the day Nature provides her own solution to the problems created by man.’” quoted a third.

“I’ve been in constant contact with Dr. Stanof and she has only fine-tuned the numbers by a few ticks. And I have the utmost respect for the Swami Bahrat. We’ve collaborated on many texts exploring quantum biology and telekinesis.” Moving to the chair behind her desk, Claudia paused to look at the pictures of Nia, Hope and Ahi sitting among her familiar things. “The longer this takes the more dire it becomes, and we are working without a net, or proper funding, or political support, or even enough sleep! But we must continue asking more questions. Is there a way to create movement of the plates and restore the field with one apparatus?”

“Well the Tsar Bombs moved the plates.”

“Ok. While I don’t advocate the use of more explosives in this already fragile ecosystem, that is just the kind of thing we need to be spit balling here. But I need you to think more creatively, more consciously." Claudia remembered, "We had a mate at university whose mother was an awful alcoholic. Started drinking when her husband passed and was killing herself with it by the time my friend started school. One Christmas, we had to go get her and put her in hospital to dry out. I watched this young girl, not yet twenty, treat her mother with such honor and respect. She knew if she didn't help her to correct the situation, she'd lose her to the drink. So we gently and kindly encouraged her to repair herself for the good of the family. It was so tender and so noble." Claudia returned from her memory to notice the solemn faces of her charges. "So that is how we must handle Mother Gia. We must go quietly, respectfully, honorably. It's not too late to show her we're sorry and we love her."

"Come on, mates, the statisticians have the final computations from the last trial, let's get back to the lab and start going over the data."

"No." They all froze, looking very surprised at their mentor. "No more tonight. You have lives. You have families, friends, partners. Go home. Eat, sleep, have sex. Leave it for the weekend. We will begin again on Monday."

"But the timeline?"

"We must continue to try to beat this timeline. A fresh perspective will be easier to work from next week. If Dr. Stanof and the Swami Bahrat are right, we have at least thirty more months to crack this. If we run out of time before Monday…that's on me." She smiled, a rarity for the group, and they erupted into exhausted laughter. Each one of these brilliant people, the obsessive-compulsives, the chronically cynical, the kiss-asses, even the germophobes and the socially inept crossed the room to shake her hand or hug her before they exited her office. She watched them empty out into the hall beyond, then crossed to the heavy wood blinds at the window and watched them as they trickled into the parking lot below and drove away into the darkness. She noted how they escorted one another to their cars, stopping to talk and shake hands or embrace before taking their leave of each other. They were a fine group of humans who not only worked well together but who also obviously cared a great deal for one another and her. She knew they wouldn't be able to completely leave the research behind, but she also knew they needed to be present in their own lives to be prolific enough to solve these problems. It was the eating and sleeping and sex that they all wanted to go on and she hoped these things that made life, *life* would inspire them.

She took her place at her desk again and called home for a check on her wife. Joffrey reported that they had a good day and that Ahi retired just after supper with the message to wake her if Claudia called. She overrode that directive with her own, making Joffrey promise not to disturb her. She said that she'd be a while longer and that he shouldn't wait up for her. She'd call a car for a ride to the flat and she'd make herself an egg sandwich when she got home. She ended the call and sat idly for a moment staring at the volumes of antiquated books inhabiting the shelves that lined the room. All this information gathered from diverse disciplines from everywhere around the world at their fingertips and still no one could solve this puzzle. "Why?" she asked aloud. "What are we missing?" The phone interrupted her self-interrogation. "Dr. Dereksen."

"Claudia, its Nia."

"Hello, my dearest. How are you and what are you doing up so early on a Saturday?" Calculating the time difference, "It's what, seven in the morning there?"

"We're grand for now. Hope and I are going on another of our all-day hikes today. How are you and Ahi? I'm not interrupting your dinner, am I?"

"No, not at all. I'm still at the lab and I just called home to check and Ahi and Joffrey are in for the night."

"Is she doing alright? It's a little early for bed already, isn't it?"

"She's not lasting as long these days, love. She is eating well, and she is getting out for her walks a few times a week, but if she doesn't rest through the day, she's in the sack by eight and nine lately."

A short silence on both ends was ripped in two by a sudden burst from Hope. "Aunt Claud! I'm transcendental!"

"What's this, Hope?" She grinned, "You're transcontinental?"

"No, transcendental! I've learned the art of meditation! You know that they introduced yoga and meditation to my group at the Institute this month and it only took me and the girls like two sessions to reach this incredible transcendental state and it was so amazing!"

"Nia, is this true? Who do you have working with them? Remdev? Sri Sri Ravi? You have to be careful when exploring consciousness."

"Yes, Claudia, I know. They are studying with Swami Bodhi Bahrat."

"Incredible! We were just talking about Bodhi. But transcendence, Hope Darling, you have probably not attained true transcendence after just a couple of sessions. Monks in Tibet meditate twenty-three hours a day for years and sometimes don't achieve true transcendence."

"Swami Bodhi says we are all conduits of prana but that the Frigus Filiae are like mystical throughways for spiritual energy. He said he was drawn to us even before he was asked to participate."

"It's Bodhi Bahrat, Claud. He's the real thing," Nia defended.

"Yes of course, I was just saying I helped him write his last two books. I am aware of how real the Swami Bahrat is."

"Aren't you pleased, Aunt Claudia?" prodded Hope.

"Pleased? She asks if I'm pleased. I'm delighted my sweet. What a gift! Congratulations, Hope. You must call Ahi when you return from your trip and share your news with her."

"I will and I need to thank you both for the book of essays you sent me. Joan Didion is my new favorite!"

"That is a rave review! Did we unseat *The Giving Tree*?"

"Ok, second favorite."

"Yes, darling. You know Ahi met Joan years ago and has a delightful story about her."

"What? Well now I have to call her and find out everything! Love you!"

"Love you!" Claudia paused then began again. "Nia, is she off?"

"Yes."

"So, what do you think?"

"I think my daughter is luminous with joy, Claudia. I don't care if she's reached nirvana or not. This practice is good for her soul and she loves it."

"And the others?"

"They are all enjoying the benefits of meditation."

"Then explain yourself, child."

"What's that now?"

"Exactly, when I asked how you were you said, 'Grand for *now*.' What are you worrying over, Nia?"

"Mmmmmm," Nia hesitated with a humming growl. "Alright, I wasn't going to tell you because I'm not even sure I saw it, but I think I saw something in the video of the last session."

"An aura?"

"No. It was movement."

"An inanimate object?"

"Not exactly… their hair."

"What? Who's hair? The girls? Had to be, Bahrat's bald as a wheel of cheese."

"The very ends of their hair turned upward and then ever so slightly swayed for a minute or two." Reeling in her speculation, Nia continued cautiously, "It's probably nothing but I am sending you the video just to see if you notice it too."

"Air conditioning, vents, fans, open doors?"

"Right, probably some totally plausible air current present. You're probably right. I'm being daft."

"But…?"

"Uggghh! Claudia, I hate your third degree sometimes!"

Claudia chuckled then pressed, "But what, Dr. Bomani?"

"But, Hope and the girls all reported having the same thought about their hair. They were not prompted or lead by Swami to visualize any one thing, but they all visualized their hair *dancing*. They were interviewed separately and without interaction with one another following the session and every one of them reported that they were concentrating on their dancing hair."

"See, I told you quantum biology is fascinating. It sounds like they are starting to learn the potential of those overactive pineal glands."

"Right. And to that end the results of the sleeping MRIs of their brains were conducted and the data concluded that their pineal glands are now operating at 100% higher levels than any other recorded human activity. They are each engaging every lobe, every cell of one of the most mysterious brain regions in our biology."

"Do not start obsessing over this, Nia. You said yourself that Hope was luminous with joy. What could be better?"

"We've worked so hard to limit the mystical appearance of these girls so that they could lead normal lives without being targeted by fear. And now this shit starts. You're the expert here. What do you make of it?"

Claudia sat silently for a moment and then released a sigh. "These are curious developments, and these are some incredible young women, but I do not have the energy to delve into this tonight. Send me the video and a sample of the MRI reports and I'll try to call Bodhi this weekend to explore the possibilities."

"It's getting harder and harder to operate strictly as the researcher. This is my daughter. And Claudia, you should see her. Her skin is gleaming like she's swallowed a torch. She looks so alive!"

"She is alive. And so are you. You had that same soul-shine the first day I saw you on tour with your class in the lab. Your light is rubbing off on your daughter. Keep her in class with the guru and enjoy her joy!"

"Yes ma'am. Good advice. I'll leave you now, you must be tired, and you've still got to get home. Give my love to Ahi and Joffrey and call us later on this weekend. Love you, Claud."

"I love you, Nia darling. Good night." She sat for another silent moment and then returned her gaze to the volumes in the wall. "Nothing in there about these little girls. That much, we know."

The Evolution 2040

"I feel so gross, Mom. Do I have to go to clinic today?" Hope, petulant in her menarche, had become increasingly irritable and fatigued. And as she had at every milestone, Nia was worried that the shift in hormones could signal some ominous turn in her daughter's health or development.

"All the more important to get your labs and scans, Hope Darling. As I told you, a little malaise and some crankiness are to be expected but I want to check your iron levels to make sure you're not anemic."

"God! This day is going to be just another boring waste!" Hope whined.

"The labs won't take long and you enjoy waiting on scans with the other girls." The two finished readying and stood side by side in front of the hall mirror. Squeezing her daughter's slender shoulders Nia consoled, "It only lasts a week, my girl, and every woman has to endure it. So let's do with a little less of this carrying on and get to actually carrying on, shall we?"

Instantly aware of your coarseness, Hope auto corrected, "Sorry, Mom."

"No worries, baby." A kiss of her oily forehead and mother led daughter out the door and into the car.

At the lab, the staff had begun the usual phlebotomy with the girls who'd already arrived when Nia poked her head in and ordered the techs to add serum iron levels to the routine tests for any of those who'd begun to menstruate. She returned to the waiting room with the other parents, a practice she was faithful to for both Hope's sake and her own. She was emphatic about preserving the equity of all the children in her research groups and with her own daughter being counted among the Cold Daughters, she insisted on participating as a parent-child dyad as well as the scientist conducting the research. She and Hope benefitted so delightfully by this inclusion. She had fostered many friendships among the parents and Hope and her cold sisters had become the darlings of the Institute. At every testing interval, the girls gathered in clumps of chatty giggling and shared and compared life stories from their unique perspective. Nia always felt uplifted by the energy they generated when they gathered in the halls of the various clinics they visited.

After her blood was drawn Hope accompanied her mother down to the basement level of the Institute for her appointments in CT and MRI. These tests required IV dyes to be administered prior to examination and so they could continue to keep one another company, the staff had retracted the dividers usually in place between patients and staggered the drips so that they could test the girls in succession with a little down time between patients. The prep room was a favorite of all the girls and while the parents were permitted to stay with their daughters most felt comfortable enough after thirteen years of this routine to wait outside until the tests were completed. Nia was often needed for consultation and as such, stuck around floating in the back halls between the prep room, testing suites and the waiting area.

A dozen girls now inhabited the prep room and like a scene out of Annie, as soon as the remaining parents and the single attending nurse left the room, they silently slipped from their gurneys and collected in a circle on the floor, IV poles in tow, to sneak in a secret meditation before they were sent back to test. They sat cross-legged, tethered to the stainless-steel shafts holding the swaying bags of saline and dye dripping into their veins parked just outside the circle. They held hands and closed their eyes and began the deep, low vibration the Swami Bahrat taught them. "Ooooommmmm."

Nia had just passed the phone back to a dad who'd been showing the group pictures of his prize-winning wolf hounds when the radiologist popped her head into the waiting room and requested her attention in the MRI suite. Nia excused herself and left the bragging man to the rest of the group. She followed the doctor through the heavy doors into the control room just outside the chamber housing the huge doughnut-shaped mechanical scanner. She glanced through the glass separating the spaces towards the empty chamber as the radiology staff explained that the machine had suddenly and inexplicably gone offline. She quizzed them about connections and asked if they'd contacted maintenance and IT. They had indeed followed protocol to the letter and nothing they attempted seemed to give them any clue as to what had happened or how to remedy the problem.

~

The nurse reentered the prep room with his coffee to find all twelve of his patients out of bed and gathered like a coven on the floor. He barked and they jumped to their feet, clambering back to their cots in a wild rush. He scolded them about being out of bed and on the floor in a hospital and they tried to hide their laughter behind their reddened expressions of shame.

~

Nia had just resigned to call the medical physicist who serviced MRIs in the Victorian territory and was about to rejoin the parents when the control panel began to beep and light up with all the signals of the appliance rebooting. She stopped and observed as the staff took note of the various steps to full operation that clipped off one and then another. After a few minutes, the radiologist looked at her and shrugged. They'd run a couple of diagnostics then proceed with testing the girls if Dr. Bomani agreed. She did and they readied the chamber while Nia returned to the waiting room and notified her parent peers of the snafu.

~

Once the nurse had properly evaluated each girl's intravenous connection and flow, he announced that he was departing again but only for a moment to see why the radiology staff had not yet come for the first patient. He warned the girls of his wrath should he return to find them out of bed again and spun through the doors into the corridors beyond. As soon as he was out of sight, the group poured from their cots and reassembled their round. They had only begun to "om" when their keeper made it to the MRI suite.

As the imager had suddenly gone offline again, the radiologist exited the control room to retrieve Nia just as the nurse was swiping his badge to enter. The staff that remained initiated the proper referrals and explained to the annoyed nurse, "You can't call the Simspon repair man when you're MRI breaks down, you need a physicist."

"It's just as well," replied the nurse, "because these imps aren't having it today, anyway." Nia had returned to hear the last of his statement and asked what he meant. "The lot of them were sitting around on the floor in their gowns like a bloody crop circle, chanting!"

"Are they doing that now?" Nia probed.

"They'd better not be. I told them there'd be hell to pay if they did it again."

She commanded the staff, "Don't touch anything." and bolted from the room with the nurse on her heels.

"It's not my fault, I'm one man and there're twelve of them!"

"No one's blaming anyone for anything."

"All the same, I'm saying we could use more staff when…"

Nia held up a hand to silence him as the two stopped short at the monitored station just outside the door to the prep room. She motioned for him to log in to the computer and swipe up the surveillance camera and she watched as the image of the inside of the room came up. There sat the dozen young people quietly meditating in a ring on the floor, hands clasped looking as peaceful as could be. She instructed him in whispers to save the data from that precise moment and to wait exactly five minutes more and break up the meditation again. She left him to it and returned to the control room with a static in her nerves that she'd never felt before. She watched as the last of the five minutes ticked by, and then just as she suspected, the idle control panel began all indications of restarting once again.

For the sake of her own satisfaction, Nia requested the series of events be repeated twice more before calling the tests and dismissing the subjects for the day. She instructed radiology to indeed have the MRI machine serviced and to reschedule all testing for after the apparatus had a clean bill of health. And while the objective data conjured suspicions, she explained nothing to nursing or radiology about the connection she felt patent between the machine's malfunction and the energy emitted by the girls' group meditation. She asked Hope what she was thinking about during the event and was met with a salty, "That I wish I didn't have to do this, Mom!"

The next day the machine was examined and cleared for use and another group of twelve girls was prepped for examination. This time, Nia had invited the Swami into the prep room and arranged mats in a circle on the floor to accommodate the deliberation. She observed them in a guided meditation, with a common visualization of being excused from testing that day. This time, the machine was unaffected. The following day she arranged for the same test with a third group and then a fourth the day after that, but none of the trials yielded results like Hope's group.

She sat ruminating in her office, her frustration getting the better of her when the phlebotomy lab called with the results of several of the girls' tests. She swiped her screen up to view the reports herself, while the physician in charge of laboratory services explained that none of the subjects' serum iron fell outside of the normal parameters but that they were all displaying higher levels of HDL cholesterol. Noting that this could mean an increase in other metal compounds in the blood, he added a complete heavy metal panel to be drawn on each girl. And it was in those panels that he found an increase in the levels of chromium circulating in their blood streams. Some he noted were close to if not at the highest therapeutic level and would need close monitoring as the research was insufficient in determining what damage the body could sustain if levels were to reach that of toxicity. She gazed at the pages of test results, flipping from patient to patient as she thanked her colleague for his thoroughness and asked to be left to consider the results of his work.

"What the hell is this all about, girls?" Nia asked herself out loud. "Ok. Group number one." She minimized the labs and brought up the charts on all twelve girls in Hope's group. The profiles appeared in the hologram as images of manila folders with their names and birthdates displayed in the upper margin. She swiped *all open* and began with the inside cover of each chart where a she found a bank of profile pictures of the child at each annual testing interval. She followed the growth of the first subject, Anele, as she tracked the images from her newborn photo all the way through to her thirteenth and present one. She noticed her perfect skin and the teeth emerging and disappearing and then returning in her sweet smile and of course she took note of the ghostly keyhole pupil in her one blue eye. Her focus lingered on the girl's white pupil for a moment more when she turned to Hope's chart to compare. The orientation of the sectoral abnormality of her daughter's right eye was horizontal. But that of Anele's was vertical. Nia had not remembered ever noting this in any other observations of these girls. Curious now to distraction, she compared the charts of the remaining ten in the initial group and one by one discovered the contrast repeated. Six girls had vertical orientation and six, horizontal. She swiped the charts down and brought up the videos from the meditation session inside the MRI prep room. She played the video of the children sitting hand in hand in a circle emitting their low vibratory mantra. She paused the action and with her finger identified each girl in the ring.

"Hope, Agnes, Celyse, Joyanne, Helena, Adiratna, Dinda, Anele, Elsea, Nova, Tessie, Gelisa." And again, around the ring, "Horizontal, vertical, horizontal, vertical, horizontal, vertical, horizontal, vertical, horizontal, vertical, horizontal, vertical." Nia rose slowly from her seat to eye the image of the girls at close range, "Interesting pattern." She brought up the next group's files and then their video. "Jozefina, horizontal next to Scarlett, horizontal next to Bente, vertical next to Tilda, also vertical next to Amisha, vertical next to Diah, again vertical next to Christabel, horizontal next to Meiko, horizontal next to Rei, also horizontal next to Herlina, again horizontal next to Anita, horizontal next to Narelle, vertical." She paced away from her desk and the projected images. "The same number of girls, but not the same ratio of vertical to horizontal or alternating pattern." She examined the third and fourth groups and still group one, the girls who disabled the imager, remained the only ones who demonstrated this alternating sequence. She thought back to the dancing hair video and pulled it up to examine those subjects' files. "Ok. There's Hope again who we know is horizontal. And Angkasa is vertical. She is next to Mustika, horizontal. She is next to Hazel, who is vertical. She is next to Ada, horizontal. Then Willow, vertical, Alice, horizontal, and Pearl, vertical. Evie is horizontal. Jondi is vertical. Olja is horizontal and Taleigha is vertical." She backed away again. "Equal number of horizontal and vertical *and* the alternating pattern." Nia drew closer and as if discovering a ghostly ether in the image, pointed to each girl in succession and whispered, "Negative, positive, negative, positive, negative, positive, negative, positive, negative, positive, negative, positive." Her face felt numb. "And chromium…they made a magnet."

She resisted the urge to call Claudia straight away. She needed more trials, more evidence, more proof. The children needed to be arranged in the same patterns as they were when they were gathered in the prep room and dancing hair sessions. It was their alternating polarity that had magnetized the chromium within them to create a field strong enough to knock a giant MRI machine offline. And this combined with the girls' collective visualizations had the power to move their hair in one session and interrupt the wireless signals to the machine in the other. She studied the environment within the prep room, mostly stainless-steel components in the equipment and furniture, so those things would not be affected by the creation of a magnetic field. And similarly, the classroom at the Institute where they studied with the swami. She couldn't keep it contained another minute, she knew this was not just a random development, this meant something. She needed Claudia's help.

The Transition 2040

Nia tapped her earpiece and commanded, "Call Claudia." When her number went straight to voicemail she disconnected and called her office. Her assistant informed her that Dr. Dereksen had not come in because of a family emergency. Nia's breath caught in her chest, Ahi. She no sooner got off the phone than it rang back. "Claudia, how is she?"

"We've had a rough night. She had been complaining of new low back pain for the last ten days or so, but she refused to go in. She kept saying she needed to drink more water and that she needed to move around a little more." Nia listened silently as Claudia took a breath and continued, "Yesterday it got so bad that I insisted she call her oncologist. He told her to go straight to hospital and he would scan her, and we'd go from there."

"And she was livid?"

"And she was livid. My God this woman is pig-headed! Now if this was you or me, she'd have us hogtied and dragged in against our will but she was going to see if a hot bath and a pain pill helped before she went all the way down town and sat around in the emergency department." Nia smiled. "Well she got in the tub and I couldn't get her out. I had to wrap her in her robe and Joffrey had to scoop her up and carry her to the car. She was a mess."

"So they admitted her?"

"Her doctor met us in the ER and said that she was dehydrated and that her labs were sufficient for admission even without the results of the PET scan. So, we went up to the tenth floor and they hung fluids and filled her full of Demerol to ease the pain and she finally fell asleep just before they came to take her to x-ray. She was down there for less than an hour and they brought her back up, sound asleep. It's the most rest she's had in days."

"So has the doctor been back in yet?"

"No, the nurse said the tests were flagged 'stat' so the radiologist would read them right away and her doctor would be up as soon as he received the report."

"You must be exhausted."

"I'm beat. And Joffrey's a mess. He keeps breaking down in tears and darting off to compose himself."

"Aw, poor Joffrey. He's such a softy."

"Ugh! He's killing me."

"I wish I would have known. We could have come out to help."

"It's been such a hectic few weeks, I honestly didn't have time to call and of course Ahi wouldn't have wanted you to worry. How is Hope's iron level? Has she gotten over her initiation into womanhood?"

"I have so much to tell you but there'll be time for all that later. We need to concentrate on you and Ahi now. I will check flights and make arrangements to get out there tomorrow or the next day and I'll bring all the new data with me so you can help me decipher it."

"*That* sounds intriguing. But there's no need to rush out here until we know what we're dealing with."

"It will do you good to have a little help and it will take Ahi's mind off things to have Hope around."

"Here's the doctor, Nia. Can I call you back?"

"I love you, good-bye." Nia ended the call and put her hand to her mouth. She tried everything to keep from crying but the tears came anyway. Who was she to admonish Joffrey for being soft? She hadn't heard a word of news about Ahi's cancer that didn't reduce her to tears every time. She wiped her face and thought about what a flat affect she had had during her childhood, the result of the violent loss of her sister and separation from her parents. She was nearly into her twenties before she began to show real emotion. And although therapy had done so much to that end, it was Claudia and Ahi who enabled her to feel safe and comfortable enough to express herself. Now she sat, alone in her office, with a knot in her guts not only for Ahi and Claudia but for Hope and the girls too. The timing was awful for this breakthrough with the Cold Daughters, but she needed Claudia's guidance and collaboration. If they could manage to get Ahi home and stable, the work would serve as a convenient diversion to keep Claudia from crashing. She was startled out of her obsessive planning when the phone buzzed in her ear. "Let's have it, what did he say?"

With a heavy sigh that signaled the worst, Claudia began, "Seven new neoplasms."

"Where?"

"Two in her right kidney, one in her left and four in her spine."

"And treatment?"

"He is not too optimistic that there's a treatment that could do anything. The osteosarcomas that responded to bone-building last year have grown since her last scan. And chemo needs two healthy kidneys to filter the blood and keep the body from toxicity. I'm not sure what's left that she hasn't already tried. He's coming back later in the morning and we'll discuss the options then."

"Claudia, are you prepared for what will happen if she doesn't want to keep up the fight?"

"I've always said that it's up to her. I would never try to sway her one way or another. And I know she's tired." The aging woman began to cry, "But no, I'm not ready, Nia. I don't want to let her go."

"You know she loves you more than anyone in this world. She would never give up just because it got difficult." Now they were both in tears.

"She hasn't so far."

"But this time, she may be too tired. We know she's weak and in considerable pain. She has fought something or other her entire life. It might be time to let her lay her weapons down and surrender. Of course, she won't put it like that."

"I've said those very words to her myself, Nia and surrender is not even in her vocabulary." The two women laughed gently now in agreement. "Would it be too much trouble for you and Hope to come?"

"I told you, we'll be out of here tomorrow. Hope's just started third term break. We're coming."

"I do think that would be good for us. We need to be together when these decisions are made."

"I'll call you later with our plans. In the meantime, stretch out and grab a nap before she wakes up. You need to take care of yourself. You still have to help me with the Frigus Filiae, lots of new developments to examine." They exchanged their love and turned their attention to what came next.

In preparation for leaving the clinic, Nia reviewed each girl's profile photos, marked them negative or positive and instructed Marjorie to schedule the rest for their scans ensuring that the groups they were gathered in were only one or the other. If her theory was correct, there would be no magnetic interference if the polarity of each group was all the same. Even though the research was taking a significant turn and Nia would need the board's unanimous support if she was to introduce new testing, she met with the chairman and asked for the short leave she needed to get to her family. The presiding officer granted her leave with the promise of a private meeting to be scheduled on her return for Nia to inform the board of the latest data on the girls. Rumors were beginning to circulate that were making the board nervous and they wanted to be kept up to date. With the dates and times agreed upon, Nia and Hope left for London.

~

The car pulled away from under the hospital canopy depositing mother and daughter before the great doors. Hope took Nia's hand and for a moment, she was an innocent child again, reaching for that safety that comes when you're not quite sure of what's to come and you need your mom to anchor you going forward. Nia squeezed, happy to be holding on to her girl for that same strength. They arrived on the tenth-floor ward and approached the room with solemn quiet. But the sounds coming from within were anything but hushed. They entered through the open door and found Ahi, Joffrey and Claudia in uproarious laughter.

"What's so funny?" Hope jumped in.

"Hope Darling!" Ahi beamed, "My loves! Come in. Joffrey just told us a joke and disabled the two of us. Oh, tell the girls, Joffrey. Tell it again!" The hulk, now crimson with embarrassment, shrunk in the attention and shaking his head vehemently, made a hasty exit leaving the room in shambles.

"Oh my God! Who knew he was that funny!" Claudia wiped tears from her face as her breath caught up to her only to erupt into her wheezing laughter all over again.

"Jesus! It must have been a doozy!"

"Hope!" Nia scolded, "Do you really think you need to bother Jesus with all this?"

"Mom lighten up. If Joffrey after all these years has a sense of humor, Jesus probably does too."

"Oh girls, it's so good to see your faces!" Ahi reached for the women and after hugs were traded and the laughter died down an uneasy stillness settled into the space between them. The comedic break was just that, a break. Everyone in that room knew there was little to laugh about. "So…you didn't fly twenty-two hours to see Joffrey's comedy debut, did you, girls?"

"We came to see you, Ahi."

"Sweet Hope, you came to get the gloom and doom report." The group sat still. "Well, it's as bad as you think. We're throwing in the towel."

"So no surgery?" Nia probed.

Ahi returned the volley, "They won't risk it."

"And radiation?"

"Won't touch it."

"And chemo?"

At once acquiescent and resigned Ahi answered, "I can't endure anymore of that poison." The air around her got too dense to manage and she took a deep, cleansing breath to scrub off its heft.

Claudia took over, "So, we've contacted Hospice and she'll be going home in a few days to get settled in. Right my love?"

"And we are all in agreement that this is what's best, aren't we, Claud?" Ahi prompted her wife.

"Yes, ever in charge, this is your call."

"Ahi, we'll do whatever you want," Nia agreed.

"But not if it's boring!" Hope declared.

"That's my Hope! Yes ma'am! We are going to embrace this last hoorah with all the zest life has to offer!" The girl snuggled up to her beloved aunt and the two began making plans.

~

After nearly another week, discharge from the hospital and the admission evaluation with her hospice nurse was smooth and uneventful but it still tired out the patient. Once the equipment was set up and the schedules for medications and nursing visits were established the nurse left the flat and Joffrey went for dinner supplies. Hope and Ahi lay in bed watching an old Barbara Stanwick movie and Claudia found Nia in the kitchen making tea.

"That went well." Nia graded.

"I'm so grateful that you two were here for this. It has been a blessing having Hope around to keep her spirits up."

"I'm glad we're here too. And I am doubly glad that Ahi has taken this route. Hospice will let her lead and her *life* can be more than just anticipating her *death*."

"Well said. Now, do you think we can talk about something besides death and cancer and hospice?"

Handing her the tea, Nia started, "I don't want to discuss this around Hope but the new development with the girls is…hell, I don't know what it is."

"Ok, let's go into the office where we can work." The two slipped into the sunny room and Nia crossed to the windows to draw the heavy drapes. The holograms were easier to view when there was less natural light. "Oooo, this looks serious."

"I want to show you the videos of the girls, but I also want to bring up their files."

"So you didn't answer me about the iron level before, normal?"

"Yes, but not the chromium level."

"Chromium?"

"But that's not all." Nia spent the next several hours outlining everything she learned about the girls and the polarity they demonstrated. The two discussed the tests she'd done, and the ones Claudia proposed she undertake when she returned to the Institute. They deliberated over every aspect of the girls' health and what the consequences of this latest development could mean.

"Nia," Claudia spoke slowly as if the idea was unfurling before her and the weight of it would crush them both if she hurried. "I think I know what to do." Nia knew too what Claudia did. But neither of them wanted to be the ones who knew. Neither of them wanted to be the ones to use what they knew to go forward. And instantly they both understood that they had to be.

Their discussion was interrupted by Hope calling them to dinner. They were rescued for the moment from the knowing.

Ahi insisted that they all gather around the table for the meal. She moved in measured steps to the dining room but arrived under her own power and was made comfortable enough to sit upright for the duration of dinner. Neither Nia nor Claudia spoke of the Cold Daughters, encouraging Hope instead, at every turn in the conversation, to entertain them with the latest stories of senior school life and the adventures they'd had on their hikes. The mismatched family sat happily in the warm glow of the lamplight well into the evening, drinking in one another's love and attention. The gathering broke when Nia's phone signaled a call from the Institute. She excused herself to take it and the table was cleared, retiring the rest of the group to the parlor.

When she returned to her family, her expression could not mask the grave news she had received. "I'm afraid we have to leave in the morning, loves."

"Aw, Mom! Why?"

"There's an emergent situation at the Institute with some of the girls and I need to return right away."

"We were going to invite Barrett over tomorrow. Why does it always have to be you to drop everything and come running every time there's something going on?" Hope challenged. "We have a life and family too, you know!"

Claudia sensed the ominous tone in Nia's voice and sustained the teen's objections, "Don't be selfish, Hope! If there is trouble for one of your sisters there's trouble for you all. You'll see Barrett on your next visit." The young woman was instantly remorseful and reached for her mother's hand.

"Aunt Claud is right, Hope Darling. You've seen us through our latest rough spot, and you're needed elsewhere now." Ahi reached for the girl, "Come on. Come spoon with me for our last night together and let your mum and Auntie Claud take care of their business."

The eldest and youngest shuffled off to bed arm-in-arm and once Joffrey retired to his room, Nia and Claudia resumed in the privacy of the study. "What is it?" began Claudia.

"Julieth, Indira and Diana have all been hospitalized with multiple organ failure. Their chromium levels are rising and it's shutting their bodies down."

"What can be done?"

"They are dialyzing them to try to reduce the levels in the blood, but we have no way of knowing if that will work or for how long."

"Multiple organ failure. I can only imagine how much pain they must be in."

"They are the Frigus Filiae, Claudia. They may be in pain, but they are not suffering."

"I'll put the kettle on. You get your boarding passes for the flight home. And we'll go over the videos and charts again. We'll get you back to your Cold Daughters with a plan of action."

Morning broke and the light creeping in between the heavy drapes in Ahi's room streaked across the sleeping Hope. Ahi stared at the young woman with the same loving eyes she had seen her through since she was a baby. Now, face to face with her own mortality, she was unable to escape the heartache of leaving her precious family. And she was suddenly aware of an aura of the same for her beloved Hope Darling. A strange foreboding produced a single tear that escaped from her eye and disappeared just before Hope's mystical eyes opened. "Good morning, Brilliance!"

"Good morning, Auntie. How did you sleep?"

"Very well thank you, love. I'll miss cuddling with you when you're gone."

Hope instantly calculated that leaving this time meant seeing her loving aunt for the very last time in this life and she was flush with grief. But the same mechanism in the nervous system of all the Cold Daughters that dictated their calm demeanor kicked in and in the next instant she was completely at peace. "I know that everyone wants to shield *the kid* from the bad stuff, but I know what's happening."

"You do?"

"I know you're dying, Ahi. And I know that changes are coming for me too."

"So how are you feeling about all this then?"

After a long pause the young woman began, "I had a dream that there was a giant ball of shining, metallic yarn. A ball of yarn bigger than the universe. And I was a strand of that giant ball of yarn and I carefully unraveled and wound around other strands out in space. Yours, Mom's, Auntie Claud's. Until I reached all the way across to Earth. And where I attached to this life, my body was formed. And there was my family. But I never let go of the yarn. I felt like I remained connected to it through my whole life. It made me…me. I was aware of myself. And then one day, when my body couldn't stay, you know, connected here anymore, it just quietly let go of the yarn and my strand traveled back out to become a part of the big metallic ball again."

Ahi gathered the girl in her arms and held her close. "I love that dream, Hope Darling." They lay in silence just being and then Ahi said, "You have created such love and joy in this life, Hope. And no matter how long we are tethered by our strands to this place, love and joy are the very best things we can leave behind when we go back to the big ball of yarn."

Hope exited first, leaving her aunts with full hearts and carried the luggage to the car. After she and the crying Joffrey loaded the bags, she held the faithful man in her young arms and his tears sputtered and stopped and he felt truly comforted by her open heart. Nia kissed Claudia and promised to call when she got to clinic and now stood holding Ahi's hands in hers, trying to remember every nuance of her beautiful matriarch. Her moody eyes, her sparkling smile, her graceful hands and her loving heart. This diminutive lady had been her savior and strength throughout her whole adult life and they both knew better than to pretend this wasn't the end. Neither would concede to it and neither could deny it. So they stood, silently reading one another and all the love and respect they had for each other. Nia's heart was overwhelmed with the grace of gratitude and she finally and simply uttered, "Thank you, Ahi." They held one another for the moment, for a lifetime and then parted. Hope and her mother held on to each other and looked back at the terrace door as the car drove away, but the curtains didn't move.

"They're just doing what comes next, Mom." Hope consoled. "Now we have to prepare ourselves for the same." What was left unspoken between them filled the silent ride to Heathrow and the long flight home. Nia's mind was beginning to grasp the scope of their situation. Something she was sure that Hope and her sisters already knew.

The Beginning

Nia finished her rounds of the latest infirmed girls, finally meeting with her family at Indira's bedside. The hemodialysis was only offering temporary relief. As soon as the process was complete, their bodies were producing more chromium. They could only endure the process three times a week and every time they commenced treatment, their organs' functions started out further and further below the normal limits. They were dying. The families of the ailing girls were not angry or depressed but predictably tranquil. But the girls themselves seemed uncomfortable with the passivity of their state.

Indira asked, "Is there not something more we can be doing, Dr. Nia?"

"The dialysis is all we can offer, Indira. We are doing everything we can."

"No ma'am, not you. Isn't there more *I* can be doing? I still feel well in between treatments. And I just feel like there is something else I need to do."

Similar requests were coming in from all the sick Daughters. It wasn't unusual for terminal patients to experience something akin to a sort of helplessness and the desire to take control of their situation. And even though she felt this wasn't exactly what the girls were expressing, Nia would soon understand completely. She dispatched the Swami Bodhi Bahrat to each of the girls in an attempt to help them gain acceptance and perspective. He was glad to comply but ultimately discovered that neither the girls nor their families lacked perspective. There was a universal acknowledgement of their fate. But this question of what *else* they could be doing continued to percolate.

The Chairman of the Board was calling for answers, but Nia had to put him off until she could get Claudia there to present their findings. "The chromium levels of the remaining girls are climbing. Scores more of them have become ill since I've been back. It's happening, Claudia."

"Nia…"

"I know what you're going to say. I know what it means." The women sat in silence for a moment then Nia uttered it, "It's the end of their season."

"When will you speak to Hope?"

"Right away, tonight, when we get home."

Nia's long workday ended, and she drove across the campus to the library where Hope had been holed up most of the day. She collected her teen and they called in an order for takeout. Once back at the flat, they mindlessly walked through their routine. Depositing bags and shoes and swapping day clothes for soft pants and braless tees, they reconvened around the table and filled their plates. Nia opened a bottle of sweeter white wine and poured a glass for herself.

"Can I have a taste?" Hope asked, her mouth full of noodles. Her mother answered with a crooked eyebrow. "Really, Mom?"

Nia needed the liquid courage but wanted her daughter to be clear-headed when she explained things to her. She was mindful of the unfairness but stood her ground. "Hope, I need to talk to you about something, something very serious. And I don't want you to be zizzing on wine."

"Ok." The girl took a few more bites but Nia only stared at her food for a moment, put her fork down and then pushed her plate away. She gathered her wine closer and added more to the glass. "Must be serious if you need a refill to tell me."

"This is about you and your sisters." The still youthful mother searched for wisdom beyond her years to find the right words, "Hope, the last lab values you girls had showed a rise in a metal found in the blood called chro– "

"Chromium." Hope completed the word.

"Yes. You know about chromium?"

"Chromium is number twenty-four on the periodic table, I think. I had to memorize that in chemistry. Plus, I overheard you and Aunt Claudia talking in the study."

"What did you hear?"

"That we have too much of it and there's a toxic effect. Is that what's making the girls sick?"

"Yes, love. But not just sick." Nia breathed in more oxygen hoping to bolster her guts. "Hope, their organs are failing. Do you know what that means?"

"They're dying."

Nia had thought she would be the one to say it. She had dreaded using that word. But it sounded so much less threatening in Hope's voice. "Yes. We are filtering some of it out of their blood with the dialysis but that is a temporary solution. It is just putting off the inevitable. And since we've been home, more and more of the girls have become ill." She took a drink. "So, we can only speculate that…"

"That we will all get sick." Now Hope pushed her plate away and reached across the table for her mother's hands. They were cool and damp from clinging to the wine glass like a life preserver. But the minute they were wrapped up in Hope's, they warmed. "I don't know how or why, Mom, but we know. We've always known that our lives weren't going to be like everyone else's." Her mother's eyebrows softened to sympathetic now. "It's not like you're imagining it, though. It's not that we've been filled with dread or fear our whole lives. We've just always known that our paths would be different."

"Different?"

"That's not the right word…exceptional!" The girl and her mother were smiling into each other's eyes, not fully aware of the presence or purpose of the tears forming in them. "We have led exceptional lives." She gave Nia's hands a squeeze. "And we are not interested in pissing them away hooked up to a blood cleaning machine on our way out."

Nia kissed Hope's hand then withdrew from her grasp and cleared her throat. "Yes. Well, did you also overhear what Aunt Claudia would propose that we have you do?" She was feeling the wine a little and wasn't sure she asked the question she intended.

"I know that we have something to do with her project. But not because I heard you two talking. I've known that I have a purpose in this life. I've been aware of that fact for as long as I can remember. And I've known that it had something to do with Aunt Claudia. If it is to reset the natural order of things and that is what Aunt Claudia is trying to do, then I'll do it. We will do it, Mom. I cannot begin to explain this to you, it sounds so weird in my head but it's what we're here for. I can't tell you what a relief it is to finally be able to tell you. *I know*. I know this is my path. I'm as sure about this part of my life as I am about your love for me. And there has never been a moment of my life that I haven't been sure that I am loved." The girl moved from her place across the table to kneel at her mother's side and recaptured her hands, "Mom, you have given me such an amazing life full of love and respect and adventure and fun. I know we were meant for each other. I know that we deserved each other. And no matter how it ends, our life together has been everything I could have ever dreamed of. And no matter how anything ends, our love will never, ever end. Mom, we are eternal." She laid her head on her mother's lap and Nia freed a hand to stroke her black curls.

"You are the most amazing girl, Hope Darling." She raised her daughter's face and held it for a moment regarding the chance they'd both been given. She bent to kiss Hope's forehead, "What an honor it is to be your mother." The two spent the evening talking about the possibilities of the Solstice Project. They stayed up well into the early hours of the morning remembering stories of the life they shared and celebrating the good fortune they'd been granted. It empowered them both to face what came next with the courage of warriors. And Hope enjoyed her first glass of wine.

The Projects

The Film

Barrett entered the flat in his slim-fitting, deep blue dinner jacket and dapper brown shoes and bowed to one of his dates. Claudia was decked in a dark aubergine dress suit and shiny black flats, and as always, looked more beautiful than she felt. He complimented her with a gesture of raised eyebrows and a cheeky nod, and she waved him off embarrassed of the attention. "You're looking particularly handsome this evening Mr. Davies," she stroked.

"Good Dr. Dereksen, Lord knows we've had our differences throughout the making of this motion picture, but you must know that tonight is the culmination of my most important work so far."

She nodded in appreciation of his declaration and nervously began her sincere request, "I know this, Barrett. You've taken such remarkable care of Ahi and her story. And that is why I must ask you to do one more thing for us."

"Anything," he offered.

"What I'm about to tell you is not for anyone else to know. I am asking you to divorce yourself from your obligations as a journalist and commit to total secrecy."

"Claudia, you have my word. Is this to do with Nia and the Cold Daughters?"

"Yes. I want a biographical record of every girl in the research. They are all being gathered at the Huffman Institute in

Victoria over the next few weeks. I need you to get with Nia and gather all their information so that they can be recognized and appreciated for their individual place in history."

"I have asked Nia before if I could do a piece on the girls and she always turned me down. May I ask why the change of heart?"

"That is complicated. They may become a monumental part of my project, at least the ones who remain well enough to participate."

"Well enough?"

"I don't want to disclose any more until we get further along with the project. Will you please create the biographical records? It's not a documentary like Ahi's, Barrett. You won't have the extravagance of the time you committed to your film, I'm afraid. The girls are undergoing a battery of tests and you must get to them when you can in between their examinations. Nia will help you gather the information and then get it back to me here as soon as you can."

"You've got my full support."

"I'll be here until the project begins its actual building stages then I'll be off to Australia myself."

"And Ahi?"

"I'm afraid she may be too ill for the journey."

"Then may I also volunteer for another assignment?"

"What is that, dear boy?"

"I'd like to stay with her once you've gone, Claudia. I love Ahi and it has been so marvelous to have spent this time with her. I can't bear the thought of her separated from you at the…" His heart choked the words short.

"At the end?" she finished. "It's alright, Barrett. We're preparing for 'the end' every day. And it is I who would be honored to accept your kindnesses."

The young biographer suddenly looked older than he had a moment ago as his eyes darkened with sad acceptance. In the next moment, Ahi emerged from the bedroom with Joffrey only slightly supporting at her elbow. Her wife and their fine escorts watched with smiling, wet eyes as she posed first and then twirled slowly and cautiously for their approval. Her tiny frame was wrapped in a smartly tailored black silk suit with a string of common paper African beads looped thrice around her sinewy neck. Her silver-slippered toes peaked out from the hem of her sleek black trousers and her out-grown, shiny gray pixie mimicked their sparkle. Her entourage regaled her with a golf clap and exited the flat for the premier.

The limo ride to the Burton Taylor Studio was short but delightful. A champagne toast to the documentary, its subject, its creator and they had arrived. The venue was small, just intimate enough for Ahi in her declining condition. It was perfect for the debut of *A Limitless Font; The Life of Ahi Mulpuru*. The tiny theatre was filled to capacity with admirers of the eighty-three-year-old. The film was a love letter to her selfless commitment to the human experience. Every frame, every interview, was crafted through the lens of her greatest devotee, Barrett Davies. So grateful for the admiration and understanding of her life's work, Ahi stood in response to the standing ovation that followed the screening and embraced the young man who had listened and learned so very much during all the hours of research they had completed together. Claudia applauded with the audience, humbled to be married to the living art Barrett's piece celebrated. She was grateful for his respectful treatment of her wife's life story and for him. He too was a fine human and even though she felt she had badgered and berated him all along the way, she couldn't imagine feeling more pride than she did in the moment he and Ahi took their final bows.

Ahi had been invited to stay for the Q&A following the premier, so she and Barrett made their way up the three narrow stairs to the stage where chairs had been ushered in during the applause. The stagehands fixed the mics on their lapels and the audience engaged the panel with probing questions about the events in and making of the film. Claudia sat rapt again, watching her beloved charm the room. Barrett sat simultaneously as star struck as ever and desperately sad that this champion of life would be gone soon. He had already started to miss her.

The brief session concluded with Ahi thanking Barrett again as the two stood to thunderous applause. Once sending the filmmaker along to the after-party and exiting gracefully for home, the couple dismissed their valet and retired to their bedroom, blissfully exhausted. As they slowly undressed one another, more compassionately than passionately, Claudia reached for their pajamas, but Ahi gently took them from her and led her wife to the bed. Cancer had left Ahi less than amorous for years and Claudia never once felt rejected or unwanted because of it. They were both acutely aware of their loss of libido. Tonight though, they felt the flicker of excitement in their dress clothes and champagne. At first the two giggled like girls. Then they lay skin to skin under the warm weight of the bedding and the night and the life they had lived together. Ahi caressed Claudia's arms and shoulders. Claudia drew near to her lover's chest and tenderly kissed her neck, then her face, then her lips. They kissed for a long time, deeply and sweetly and held one another tighter and tighter. When their lips parted, they lay smiling into each other's eyes. All the life, all the love, it was right there. They saw in that instant like so many times before, that they were the lucky ones. They were blessed by the universe to have found love like no other and grateful to have had the presence-of-mind to know it from the very start. The couple slept soundly in the comfort of each other's hearts.

Claudia and Joffrey read the reviews of the film over breakfast while Ahi slept. "I'm so very pleased that the project has received such acclaim. That boy is going to do big things." Claudia pronounced. Joffrey nodded with agreement and finished his jam and toast. Tiptoeing into the bedroom before she left for the lab, Claudia found Ahi awake but not up. "Good morning, my love."

"Good morning. Oh, Claudia, I'm beat. Aren't you tired? You're up and dressed."

"Yes, Joffrey and I ate already, and we couldn't wait, we read the papers."

"Well?"

"Great reviews, Ahi. Words like 'stunning' and 'captivating'. He did such a good job."

"That is good news. I'm so relieved. I was afraid I just liked it because it was all about me!" The two laughed out loud at Ahi's narcissistic admission. "Are you off then?" she asked as they regained their composure.

"Yes, there have been new developments with the project."

"Which project?"

"With the Solstice Project and…

"And?"

"And with the Frigus Filiae. I am waiting on word from Nia and then I may have to be at the Institute until the whole thing is complete. I am going to address my team today to lay the groundwork."

The intuitive Ahi reassured her wife, "They're ready you know, Claudia."

"My team?"

"Nia…and Hope… and all the girls," she continued, "They know, and they are ready." The two fixed their eyes onto one another's for a moment and Ahi added, "And I'm ready too. You can go where you are needed. And I will be here for as long as I can. But time *is* of the essence, my love."

Claudia held Ahi's hands together over the covers and kissed them, "Never truer more than now."

~

The Field Trip

Nia gave her tablet to Marjorie and asked her to run down the roll as the last of the three dozen girls boarded the bus, assuming their assigned seats. "Please raise your hand when I call your name, girls." Marjorie complied. A collective nod waved through the tall backs of the bus seats as she began, "Isla. Grace. Willow. Audrey. Evelyn. Poppy. Sofia. Milla. Billi. Sadie."

As the bus driver pushed past her standing on the bottom step inside the open door, Nia reiterated the final plans to the parents gathered in the Institute parking lot in the creeping dawn, her words puffs of condensation in the cool morning air. "So, straight to the Acton Campus in Canberra. We should be on the road a little over nine hours. We're sticking to…" she turned to verify with the driver, "M31?"

"All the way." he announced.

"M31 all the way to ANU. I'll send out a mass text when we arrive. Oh, and when we stop along the way for lunch."

"Albury," stated the driver, programming the bus's GPS.

"There are lots of eateries along Dean Street in Albury, Dr. Nia." offered one father in the back of the group.

"Excellent, good to know. Thank you. We'll check into the dorms a little before dinner and then relax for the evening. Our session in the lab begins at nine o'clock tomorrow morning and will take the better part of the next two days.

Back in the bus, rollcall continued. "Seraphina. Druzy. Ellena. Garnet." The girls began to settle in and those whose names had been called reached for books and earbuds in their backpacks. "We've never been on a field trip before," and other similar observations were whispered between the names. "Isti. Jano. Faith. Kissma. Rika."

"If anything comes up, I will call immediately. You all have my and my assistant's numbers? Marjorie will be by my side every minute and will relay any information you may need. And of course, they all have their handhelds." A keen laughter trickled from the group. Another quick glance back to the driver earned her a wide-eyed, impatient thumbs-up and she hurried on, "So we will see you in a couple of days. Thank you all." Nia smiled and waved, and turning away from the closing door, climbed the remaining steps and inched past Marjorie who had just completed the roll and the housekeeping speech familiar to all trips on charter buses with teenage passengers. The two women settled into their seats and the girls waved to their dispersing parents out the wide, tinted windows of the Murrays coach. The air released from the bus's brakes and with a gentle lurch, the trip began.

Nia sent out a quick text to Hope who'd not been included on the roster for this round of examinations. The teen was livid she didn't get to go but Nia was relieved that the randomly generated list had not included her daughter this time. "Just off. Will you call me later and let me know what you're getting into?"

"No."

Nia frowned. "Are you serious?"

"NO."

"I love you, Hope Darling."

"Sorry for the salt. Just jelly. Have a great time. Love you too."

The group quietly hummed with chatter and low music as they careened across the complex terrain of southeast Australia. The girls were pleased they would get to visit a college campus and stay in the dorms overnight. Their parents as always, were calm and reserved about the trip. Nia often imagined what it was like for them. She and Hope had a pretty normal life but her intimate connection with the research afforded her an "insider's awareness" that the others didn't possess. And yet, they consented to every query, every test, and every experiment with acceptance and trust. She believed she would be frantic if a genetic researcher had asked to take her teenage daughter nearly seven hundred kilometers away to have experiments performed on her and her friends. She knew it wasn't normal parental behavior to hand your child (especially as unique a child as one of these) over to scientists no matter what they were going to do. But these girls' families were brave and certain about their daughters' place in their lives and the bigger human family. The peace these young people possessed in their pure, weird, cold hearts had long been the source of the compliance of all the parents engaged in supporting their girls in Nia's research. Even though the tests at ANU were innocuous, she still felt relief that Hope would be spared any part of being studied by an entity outside the Institute.

Her train of thought was derailed when she was ambushed by a stealthy passenger who had silently made her way to the front of the bus, "Dr. Nia?" the wiry girl boomed over the thundering bus motor.

"Jesus!" Nia started, snapping Marjorie's head out of her paperwork across the aisle. "So, sorry, Quinn."

"No ma'am. I'm sorry. I didn't mean to startle you."

"What is it, miss?

"We just wanted to know if we could trade seats and chat for a while, just to keep from getting bored."

"Sorry Miss Quinn. We have you where you must remain for the duration of the trip." Standing she spoke to the entire vehicle. "Ladies, it is imperative that you remain in your assigned seats for the entirety of the trip. It is of the utmost importance for your safety and the safe operation of this vehicle." She had not disclosed her discovery of their opposing polarity (although she was sure in her deepest thoughts that they already knew) and she wasn't ready at this juncture to do so in front of Marjorie and the bus driver.

The bus driver looking puzzled glared at Nia through the rearview mirror. She sent the girl back to her seat and returned to her own, barely glancing up to meet his eyes in their reflection. All too curiously now, he quizzed her, "What the hell does that mean? Are they radioactive or something?"

At once both furrowing her brow and smiling, she replied, "Something." His caveman brain registered her enigmatic response as flirtatious and he triumphantly redirected his full attention to his driving. She dismissed their interaction all together and got lost in her tablet, where she had begun thoughtfully constructing her presentation to the board.

The miles disappeared under the wheels and the group arrived in Albury, roughly half-way to their destination. The girls curiously pointed out interesting shops and storefronts while the driver maneuvered the big coach through the wide streets of the town. "Dean Street." He shot a cocky smile back to Nia and pulled the bus to a stop in an open parking lot central to a row of restaurants.

"Ok, ladies. We've narrowed our choices to GreenStreat, organic-locally grown salads and sandwiches; Brick Lane, bistro selections; or the Downtown Pizzeria."

"PIZZA!!" the universal call rang out.

Marjorie grinned at her boss, "Did you really think they'd pick anything else?"

Nia surrendered and led the assembly off the bus and down the block to the restaurant. The dining hall was busy with the lunch crowd, so the travelers were ushered outside to the patio. It was already warm on the covered porch and the girls pushed wooden tables together to keep the group more compact for ordering and serving. Two waitresses began at opposite sides of the gathering, listing specials and jotting down orders. The girls popped off a few at a time to wash up and use the facilities. Nia was ever vigilant about sending them in small clumps in case they encountered any foolishness. She had lost track of the driver who Marjorie assured her had opened a brown-paper bag lunch at his seat in the bus as she followed the last of the girls out.

"I'll bet he knows exactly where *you* are, doctor." Marjorie teased.

"It's been so long since I've even entertained thoughts like that, Marjorie. I wouldn't be able to find my way with a flag tied to it!"

Giggling like one of their charges, Marjorie mused, "I wouldn't mind having a crack at that whip."

"You should absolutely go for it, sister." Nia cheered, "Just wait till he gets us back home in one piece."

Nia watched the young ladies relishing their al fresco pause, trying to enjoy her own presence in the moment and after, with full bellies and light hearts, they reboarded the bus for the final leg of their destination. The second half of the trip seemed shorter than the first and before long, they arrived at the university. Nia exited the bus alone at the Aboriginal Student Center and was met at reception by the young man who would serve as their guide and chaperone. Offering his thick dark hand, he began, "Pleased to meet you Dr. Bomani. I'm Monti." She took his hand and read a firm measure of respect in the gesture. He had a gentle, welcoming face with slender black eyes and a wide nose. His features revealed an obviously indigenous heritage, but his close fade topped with short dreads and his bushy goatee conveyed a style demonstrative of the twenty-first century.

"Monti. Black-necked stork."

"Yes!" he beamed.

"Don't ask me how or even why I know that, Monti," she diverted. "Let alone how I remember it. I can't tell you where my keys are, but I know the Aboriginal origin of your name."

"Very impressive, just the same, doctor." He was indeed impressed with Nia, not for her trivial memory but for her body of work and her connection to Claudia and *her* work as well. He was a physics major in his second year of the graduate program at ANU and the only person outside the Deputy Dean of Science to know about this round of examinations on the girls. Claudia had managed to call in a favor of the department head and the administrator recommended Monti siting his admiration for her scientific work as his driving force to assist as well as protect the project's secrecy. Nia and the young scientist exchanged packets of information and he called up the campus map on her tablet, directing her to the dorms and laboratories the girls would be occupying during their stay. He followed her out the front doors of the center and waved them on before cutting across campus on foot to meet them at their terminus.

The business of unpacking the bus and registering all the girls as guests of the college and directing them to their respective accommodations was the last bit of tedium before dinner. Nia let Marjorie and Monti accompany the group down to the dining hall without her. Alone in her room, she took the time to send the group text she promised to the parents and then called home for a quick check of her own Cold Daughter.

"Hey, Mom." Hope chimed.

"Hey, Baby. How was your day?"

"Good. Staying at Beth's house is always so cool." Hope was staying with her best friend from school who was not a Cold Daughter but the very warm daughter of a colleague of Nia's from the institute. Beth shared Hope's love of stand-up comedy, the essays of Joan Didion and the poetry of Shel Silverstein. "How about yours? How was the trip? Are you there yet?"

"Just got settled into the dorms. It's a beautiful campus."

"Was the bus ride a butt-ache?"

Laughing at her choice of words Nia responded, “Not altogether, no. It went smoothly enough, I guess. Oh! Marjorie thinks the bus driver has a thing for me. But I told her I wasn’t interested and that she should try for him, instead.”

Now they were both laughing. “She’s right, Mom. You could use a little companionship.”

“I’ve got you, Hope Darling. What better company could I ask for?”

“Gross! Mom, I’m talking about sex! You can’t possibly be satisfied in *that way* when you never hang around anybody but your thirteen-year-old daughter and her weird friends.”

“Hope, really.”

“I mean it, Mom. You need to get out there and find someone you like spending time with. I’m not going to be around forever.”

Her last words fixed them both, breathless and silent. Normal as it seemed on the surface for a teen to encourage her single mother to seek love because *her* life would be turning outwardly, away from home, when she’d be leaving for university and adulthood; there was more weight to the subject when Hope spoke about it. They both knew that a separation was imminent and neither sensed that it would be normal. Nia hoped against all that her daughter would survive the toxic end that so many of her cold sisters were already nearing and that if they were somehow designated to be instrumental in the Solstice Project that that too would be survivable. She longed for the nest emptied by Hope simply going off to school or leaving to follow love or life in any form. And with a simple kindness, calmness replaced her dread when Hope began again. “Well, anyway, I love you, Momma.”

"I love you more and more, Hope, always and all ways."

The exhausting day ended for Nia and Marjorie and the bus driver and Monti and Hope, all the Cold Daughters and the world the same way; one day closer to the solstice. The next one would be full of possibilities for everyone.

The physics lab where the girls would be examined was unremarkable. The white walls were interrupted by rectangular gray acoustic panels that mimicked the tile floor. A partial height partition occupied the near corner of the room and in it sat a waist-high machine no bigger than a teacart. It had a large copper roller fixed onto the top of its console bearing an impressive display of terminals, buttons, dials, and scribing needles poised to etch out feedback from the session. The girls had been divided into three equal groups and the first twelve were seated by alternating polarity in a circle of molded plastic chairs in the center of the room. Monti explained to Nia that when measuring faint traces of typical human magnetic activity such as heart and brain waves, this magnetometer was all they would need; that people rarely exhibited field strengths greater than 1microtesla and so would not require the employment of any equipment more sophisticated. She cautioned him that these girls were human people to be sure but that they also possessed some atypical qualities that might prove unusual in their experiments. Respectfully dismissing her caveat, he escorted her to a seat behind the knee wall and engaged the apparatus.

The girls were instructed to simply sit and relax, breathing normally and to clear their minds of any particular thought. They did, and the experiment began. The lights of the machine blinked green and the dials minimally reacted barely oscillating between -1and +1. The pen at the end of the thin armature etched the slightest zigzag hardly discernable from the flat baseline. The machine pushed a strip of paper tape out and Monti pulled it further to show Nia the low strength of the magnetism present in the atmosphere of the closed room. He switched the knobs and dials back to their neutral positions and scrawled a notation with a ball-point pen on the tape where that portion of the session concluded.

With the machine reset, he instructed the girls to join hands. Again, they were to sit relaxed, mind and body. He restarted the magnetometer. As if a surge of power had entered its motherboard, every light ignited, glowing amber, red and green, every dial flung wildly from the central zero to the furthest hashes on the right and the stylus jumped and skidded and scribbled uncontrollably while the paper tape zoomed from its feed. An audible crackle was heard in the room and the lights flickered off and on. Monti grabbed at the console and barked at the girls, "Let go!" Nia was on her feet and across the room in a flash and a thin ribbon of smoke emerged from beneath the copper roller. "Please exit the room and return to the commons with the others, doctor." The young man was breathing heavier than he meant to and Nia could see the panic on his face. She prodded the girls from their places and at once they were gone. Monti sat for a moment disconnecting leads and examining the feedback with astonishment. He definitely needed to make an adjustment, maybe many. His face spread out with excitement.

After a short break where no one was really certain of his whereabouts, the student returned to the commons area composed and apologetic. He bent to speak discretely to Nia and the same dozen girls were divided from the group and escorted down the halls of the sprawling building. This new chamber was twice the size of the original space and touted a large bank of equipment taking up the length of one wall. A similar circle of chairs appeared in the center and the girls were ushered in and positioned in the alternating pattern of their charges exactly like the earlier trial.

Nia was led to the console and Monti began presenting. "This, Dr. Bomani is a Gauss meter used to measure field strength in gauss units which compare 10,000:1 with Teslas. This apparatus is capable of measuring fields within its chamber (he gestured to the entirety of the room) of greater than 1µT and can record strengths as significant as 31.869 µT, the strength of Earth's magnetic field at 0° latitude, 0° longitude." Nia nodded with understanding at the upgrade and watched as her guide readied the mechanism.

For a baseline, he tested the young women first without holding hands to flat results, as he expected and then connecting as they had in the previous demonstration. The outcome was even more sensational than Monti predicted. Even though the capabilities of the Gauss meter enabled the experiment to be completed with less dramatic consequences, the data gathered was substantially more impressive. The apparatus recorded a field around the girls equivalent to 36 µT. The group was then tested again standing, holding hands and walking in a circle as fast as they could without falling. This produced even stronger readings from the machine. Since he was only privy to this piece of the puzzle, Monti couldn't know the impact of his findings. But Nia knew. And Claudia would know. And the girls were beginning to show signs that they too knew the significance of the tests.

The other girls spent their time between the library and the Fellows Oval across the lane from the physics campus. The space offered a cool green oasis in the middle of the vast university grounds. They read and wrote and discussed life as they knew it, soaking up the sun and as always, enjoying just being, acutely present.

The day's events saw two-thirds of the Cold Daughters tested and left only the last twelve to include in the experiments the following day. The group rose early and concluded the testing by noon. Monti surprised them with passes to a stage play presented by the school's drama department and they delighted in the live performance. Once they were safely returned to the dorms and prepared for their early departure the next day, Nia met privately with Monti and the Deputy Dean to discuss the success of the trip.

"I can't thank you enough for everything you've done for us in these two days." Nia's gratitude was sincere and received as such. "Monti, I'm sorry if we scared you at first, but you did a fine job."

The young man reddened, and he looked to his superior and back to Nia. "It was my honor, Dr. Bomani." They again exchanged their respect with another firm handshake.

"I especially appreciate the discretion you've been able to afford this whole thing."

"Yes." Monti began again, "I accept that this had to be handled with the utmost confidentiality, but are we allowed to know if our experiments were successful in proving whatever it was you were after?"

"Yes, sir." Nia answered. "Yes, you are allowed to know. And yes, we established the proof. For this, Monti, the entire world will thank you one day."

She left the young man just as curious as he was satisfied with his involvement. She was certain that his brief interaction with the girls would quietly hang in his memory for the remainder of his life, which she hoped would be decades longer. She called Claudia when she returned to the dorm and reported that their data was conclusive, and she should go forward with the plans to begin the construction phase of the project. Once there was a comprehensive plan to present to the board, Claudia would join Nia at the Institute and they would begin in earnest.

~

M.A.G.N.E.T.S.

Dr. Dereksen summoned her team and their assistants and interns to a lecture hall at St. Anne's College on the north end of the Oxford campus with all the material they had gathered to that point about the project. She began her address with the constants that every team across the globe had agreed upon, "So given the dimensions of the Weber Deep of some 7.2 kilometers deep and 60,000 kilometers wide, the fissure at its base we think, measures only another 1 or 2 deeper than that by a modest half a kilometer wide. And we know that the temperature of the water averages around three degrees Celsius, and we need a pure ore to use that keeps its ferromagnetic properties in the cold. We've known what kind of an apparatus we need to build to recreate the magnetic field. The question is, how to close the gap once the core's magnetism has been recharged in order to keep the geomagnetic field in place? We've all been attempting to engineer an appliance, a giant, artificial electromagnet powerful enough to create that kind of force *and* move the earth." She let them sit with the obvious.

"But what if nature had the answer all along?" A quiet rustling swished through the captive crowd as she began to pace. "What if there was a group of *people* who possessed either negative or positive polarity and organically produced enough chromium to create their own magnetism… and had subhuman internal body temperatures that would enable them to withstand the depths of the ocean…and displayed the collective psychokinetic powers sufficient to move the earth around them?"

One bold soul in the last row raised his hand, "Doctor, we tried chromium, but it is antiferromagnetic."

Another answered her peer, "Not when it's bathed in superfluid helium. Then it becomes ferromagnetic and can remain so in cold temperatures."

"Very good!" Claudia resumed control of the discussion, "And what does the detonation of a hydrogen bomb yield?" There was a collective response, "Helium."

"Are you presenting a hypothetical, doctor?" asked a grad student.

"No. These people exist. You know them as the Cold Daughters."

Another murmur coursed through the group and then someone else quizzed, "How many of them are there?"

"Less than two hundred remain in good enough health to withstand hazardous conditions, and we're in danger of losing more to chromium toxicity if we don't act soon."

Another professor engaged, "If we separated them into evenly polarized groups all along the edge of the cleft, and we could somehow make them centrifugally rotate at the speeds necessary to produce at or around 65 microteslas, hypothetically speaking, they could create a field that could incite the elements in the core to magnetize and protect the troposphere at the same time!"

The assembly was abuzz with conjecture now. Another member called out amid the din, "And if they use their psychokinetic connection to "mend the earth" or "close the deep" or some such intonation, oh my God! It's only five hundred meters. If they could make the earth move just five hundred meters!" A full frenzy of super charged intellect, speculation, arguments and insight erupted in the hall. Claudia felt from the depths of her soul that this moment in history was precisely the reason she had chosen her field. As much as this event marked the purpose of these unique children, it would prove to be her destiny as well.

The lab was moved to Oxford's Iffley Road Rec Complex to accommodate the mass of computers and workstations necessary for the hotbed of activity that had become the Solstice Project. The glass floors of the indoor sports courts were scored into rectangular sections by the LED lights below producing a modicum of organization in the chaotic space. Even though it was shrouded in secrecy to prevent deadly interference from anywhere outside the scientific community, teams worldwide were alerted and began communicating under the radar with Claudia's to collaborate on the specifics of every detail. She wandered the floor of the sprawling command center where designers interfaced with physicists and robotics engineers to draft plans for the machines that would make up the project. They reported to her when they met a milestone, or a snag and she directed and redirected as necessary throughout the process. The exchange of information across the globe was nothing short of miraculous and bit by bit the project's implements were coming together. With barely a moment for personal reflection, Claudia couldn't help but be repeatedly reminded of the immense pride she felt for her peers and even more so for her individual crew. She had nurtured this group throughout their graduate studies and recommended them for fellowships and in some cases even stood up for them at their weddings. They were her family and she was counting on them to fly in the face of impossibility.

A young designer pushed through the crowded floor to the doctor with hand-drawn sketches on bumwad clutched in her hands and two lanky interns crowding in behind her. Raising her hands to defend against the rush and receive the drawings, Claudia asked, "Ok, people. What have we here?"

"We call it the Mechanical Amphibious Gauss-Neutral Electrolytic Transportation System or M.A.G.N.E.T.S." spewed the designer.

“You’ve got me so far,” led Claudia.

“Dr. Dereksen, have you ever been on the Meteorite at Worden Park in Leyland, Lancashire?” asked one of the interns.

“A stranger question couldn’t be asked of me right now but yes. It’s been a hundred years ago but I think I remember that ride.”

The designer continued, “We can build six of them with twenty-four interconnected pods for a total of one hundred forty-four of the girls.”

“We know we have to use an even number of them to make the polarity work,” interjected the other intern. “We think this will safely utilize the most girls presumably creating the most energy.”

“Yes.” Claudia agreed. “One hundred forty-four out of the original two hundred thirty-three is the very best we could hope for.”

“Two-thirty-three…and one-forty-four?” The designer spoke it aloud, while the interns’ wide eyes took in the mathematic significance. “But that’s…”

“Yes, the Golden Proportion.” Claudia confirmed, “What more evidence do we need that it must be exactly as you’ve designed it? Get to it people!” The young trio looked at each other and scrambled to their computers to render the three-dimensional models necessary to begin construction of the machines.

Claudia continued on her way. She walked along the banks of cubicles until she got to the squad in charge of materials. “Where are we this morning, mates?”

Spilling out of the chairs in their station, they revealed the monitor displaying the atomic structure of a plastic compound they agreed would be the best option. One of the chemists offered, "We think by using this specific polytetrafluoroethylene to form the pods we can count on its chemical tendency to promote dielectric relaxation of the magnetic field aiding in the hysteresis that will keep the earth in her own memory loop to close the gap."

"Excellent work," she lauded. "Now get this to the architects. The engineers are working with them on the specs of the mechanisms, they'll need your input for their materials list." One remained to save the file and send the information digitally; one waited for the data to be uploaded to a flash drive then extracted it and bolted off across the crowded maze to make a physical delivery.

Claudia continued along the busy paths amid the clusters of huddled professionals approving the oxygen delivery system created by the aerospace consortium and the audio communication connections devised by the sound technicians. There were animators digitally generating what the artists had rendered in clay models on pivoting screens to share multidimensional views of how the suits the girls would be required to wear would plug into the inner lining of the individual pods in order to monitor their life support for the duration of the submersion. A hydro-aquatic gel bead was suggested as a medium for suspending the girls' bodies within each pod to equalize the deep water's pressure sure to be a threat outside the machines. Cut stone weights and milled claws would drop the machines in place and anchor them to the ocean floor and would break away after completion of the project when latex balloon-like mechanisms would deploy and incrementally inflate to gradually lift them back up to the surface.

The technical riggings were coming together systematically. Claudia had only to return to Victoria with a prototype and she and Nia could present to the board.

~

Home

At the end of the second day's testing and just before lying down to bed, Nia received a call from Barrett. He would be in Victoria tomorrow night and begin creating the girls' bios the following day. She was glad she'd be seeing him. They had developed a kinship over the time he was working with Ahi and Nia was feeling like she could use a friend.

"We're at ANU with a group of the girls tonight, Barrett. We're leaving in the morning but won't be home until late. When does your flight get in?"

"I won't be landing until eight tomorrow night myself. Is Hope with you?"

"No, not this trip. We'll see her tomorrow night though. You'll stay with us of course. We can ride into the Institute together."

"That would be perfect, thanks. Nia?"

"Yes, Barrett."

"Claudia told me a little about what's going on with the girls." There was an obvious silence. "Are you ok?"

"Barrett, that is a question I cannot even afford to ask myself right now, let alone answer."

"I'm sorry I brought it up."

"You are forgiven. Have a safe trip and we'll see you tomorrow night." Alone in the quiet of her room, she doubled down on her response to him. She could not ponder it. She could not answer it. That was the only way to be right now.

Morning came and the process of packing the bus and getting all aboard was effortless with these remarkable young people. Marjorie had refrained from advancing toward the bus driver when they stopped again for lunch but was clearly more talkative as the group approached the familiar turns near home. The evening was clear and warm, and the bus was met with quiet smiles and warm embraces from the families of each passenger. Instruction was given to report to the Institute again in the morning when a briefing of the trip's objectives would be held.

Nia dropped into her car and called Hope. Of course, she missed her, but it was already so late, and could she please stay another night with Beth. They had just started creating an animation of a rap they wrote for an extra credit project for drama class next term. How could she deny a request like that? They said their good nights and she called Barrett.

"Dinner?" he suggested, having been holding down a seat at the bar around the corner from her flat for the hour since he'd landed in Victoria.

"I'm starving! So, yes please." She arrived to find he had moved to a booth in the quieter end of the pub and had a cold draft already being delivered to her as she sat.

"You look beat."

"Thanks. That's just what a girl wants to hear when she comes home at the end of a long day." He grinned. "Hi, Honey, I'm home! – 'Oh, you look like warm shit, dear'," she chided.

“How was it? Grueling?”

“No. That’s just it. It was time consuming and I was kind of hoping we wouldn’t get where we were going but it went really well and here we are.” The waitress came and collected their orders then vanished unseen. “How about you? How was the premier?”

“Amazing! Oh my God! Amazing, Nia.” His eyes ignited with the love he had for Ahi and the sheer bliss he enjoyed during the making of the film with her. “She is my hero. It’s just that simple. And to have the chance to chronicle her life and her achievements was nothing short of my wildest dreams.”

“I know. Those two are everything to me and Hope. I don’t even want to imagine where we’d be without them.” The words pulled their meaning out of her heart and her head fell into her hands.

“Nia, you’re tired.” The waitress returned with their fare and he prompted her to box it up and bring the check.

“I’m fine.” She attempted to compose herself, but her eyes betrayed her glistening with the tears she couldn’t hold on to. “I’m fine.”

“I’ve had enough of this place for tonight.” Barrett lied. “Can we please just go?”

“I guess. If that’s what you want.” Oblivious to his bailing for her sake, she wiped her face on her napkin and gathered her purse. He grabbed the boxes of food and slipped out of the booth.

The apartment was stagnant and too dark. She opened the terrace door to circulate some fresh air and he turned on the lamps in the living room. They took the food containers and sat on the floor around the coffee table sampling each other’s choices and talking like the old friends they had become.

"I hate that we don't have Hope here." He said sincerely missing the impetuous teen.

"I know. I spent four days with everyone else's kids and couldn't wait to get back to my own, only to find that she's having more fun doing extra credit with *Beth* than getting home to see her own mom!" She chuckled but felt a tinge of real pain through the humor of it.

"She's a teenager now, Nia. You no longer hold that coveted place as the most interesting person in her life anymore."

"Look at you, Mr. father-of-the-year! What the hell would a bloody bachelor who hangs out with old ladies know about any of that?"

"I'm quite sure I have no idea where that came from. I haven't the slightest idea how you handle any of this shit. Absolutely over my head…all this."

"Right? Well at least we agree on something."

The food was cold, and the conversation was losing its frivolity. Nia was glad he was here. Glad to have someone she could talk to. She felt none of her usual loneliness for the first time in as long as she could remember. And in this safety, she began, "So, I don't know what Claudia has told you but…" She laid out the reasons for her trip to the university and the work being done at the Oxford labs and the entirety of their plans to try to use the girls in the Solstice Project.

He absorbed every word with the attention of a reporter but the concern of a family member. She got through it all without a tear. She was surprised and pleased with herself. And Hope wasn't even around to draw calmness from. Barrett had done it this time.

It was him and his careful blue eyes magnified by his thick glasses and his bristly red hair and his big, tender hands that made her feel secure enough to describe the whole arc of events.

He sat motionless, absorbing everything. His heart was broken for Nia and Hope, no matter what happened, their lives would never be the same. And with Ahi so ill and Claudia needing to be here for the project, he finally understood what he'd been tasked with; the bios and then returning to stay with Ahi; all these incredible women…and him. He was overwhelmed. While he contemplated everything, she rose and gathered the leftovers to the kitchen. She glanced back at him sitting in stillness on the couch and caught the glint of a tear escaping from under the dark frame of his glasses.

She was quick to his side. "It's a lot. I'm sorry. I probably shouldn't have dumped all that on you." With one hand she held his arm as the other instinctively rubbed his back to soothe him.

"No." he said staring past her. "You must have been going mad, keeping all that to yourself." The young man turned his face to his friend's. "How are we going to do this? How are YOU going to do this?"

Her fear of the question, of the answer poured into the pool of warm safety she felt with Barrett near her and... they leapt. Their faces connected at their lips and tongues and their hands found each other's necks and hair. She pressed him against the couch, and he pulled her over him like a soft quilt. They kept their eyes closed in case one saw hesitation in the other's glance. They felt under clothes for skin and when they found it, they reached for more. Warm, wet places came undone and he pushed into her. Their breath in sync kept cadence with the rise and fall of their hips. No words but deep, satisfying communication. Close. Home. Love.

When their breathing had returned to normal and their sweat began to cool their skin, they spooned, tangled in a throw that earlier laid over the back of the couch. Sleep came immediately for them both, without so much as a 'good night' exchanged between them. Night slipped out and conceded to the rising sun. Nia's eyes opened and she registered Barrett's heat along the back of her body. She glanced down to identify his hand as the warmth she held in hers. She whispered, "Barrett."

He inhaled her scent at the base of her neck and breathed, "Good morning."

She wriggled to her back so she could see him and smiled at his naked eyes. "What the hell?"

"Right? I know. Now what?"

"Well, I am sure I haven't the foggiest idea what we're supposed to do next as I haven't done anything like this since…ok, I've never done anything like *this*!"

"Is that an insult?" He popped up on his elbow to scowl down at her. "You mean you've never been with anyone like me?"

"I mean I've never been with anyone I loved before." Her eyes were hot with embarrassment. She knew what she meant by 'love', but she wasn't sure how that translated to him in their current position. "I mean…well you know what I mean, right? I don't need a man to …"

"Do I know what you mean by love?" He was in the arms of someone he had shared such close ties with and felt such deep feelings for, of course they loved each other. But even as he sensed her unease, he felt playful. "Are you saying you're in love with me?"

"Oh God! We've made a mistake. I'm so sorry. Not in love.

No. Barrett, I'm a feminist, I would never define myself by the love of…"

"What? I'm crushed! After everything last night and…you're not a feminist! I'm a feminist, you're just a harlot!"

She launched herself off the couch and dove into her clothes laying empty on the floor then spun around to kneel in front of the couch, squawking at his tender hands now covering his face. "Fuck! I'm so sorry. No. I don't know about 'in love'. I'm just saying. I love you!" His feigned heartbreak was replaced with his growing grin and she saw through his teasing. "You ass!" She swiped at him. She kissed his teeth through smiling lips. "Of course I love you, Barrett."

"And I love you, Nia." he answered.

"But this isn't a declaration of my love. This, we just happened. I won't be defined by who I love!"

"Why not? What would be so bad about that, Nia?" She lowered her head. "You love your daughter and that makes you a wonderful mother. You love Ahi and Claudia and that makes you a wonderful daughter. And you love me. So what? That just makes you a valuable friend. And now we have this layer of love. What could be wrong with loving your friend?"

She sat dumbfounded, speechless. All her life she tried to get by without love becoming her most valuable emotional currency and in one night, he'd unraveled her whole plan. He was right and she hated him for it. In the next instant a key turned in the front door and Hope appeared in the doorway. "Oh, Barrett!" she lilted, "Whew! I thought you were the bus driver for a minute. Morning, Mom! I had Beth's mom drop me off so I could ride in with you guys this morning. We'd better get going if we're not going to be late to the Institute." And she popped off to her room to ready herself for the day. The stunned couple sat caught and guilty for only another moment then sprang into action gathering the evidence of their night and disappearing behind bathroom and bedroom doors.

The End

Nia entered the large general-purpose room at the Institute with Barrett, Swami Bodhi Bahrat, and Hope by her side. Her friends and daughter took seats behind the folding table in the front of the room and Nia took her place in front of that. She scanned the group of parents and those of their Cold Daughters who were well enough to attend. She had invited everyone, even those whose girls were close to death. She needed a group consensus about the issues before them and she'd take every vote into consideration.

"Good morning, everyone." A subdued answer returned from the mass. "I want to thank you for coming in today. I realize it is still a hardship for many of you to travel to us and that this is an unscheduled visit. We will not be doing any new examinations on our girls. That's not what this meeting is about. As you know, many of the kids have become gravely ill, some even too ill to attend today, and still I see those of you girls who, heroically, came even though it is a dialysis day. We are here to discuss the implications of our daughters' current health threats, their unique abilities and ultimately the potential these young women possess for the future." She shifted on her feet to lean against the table behind her and Hope pushed a bottle of water toward her. She held it but did not drink.

She inhaled and began again, "First of all, the onset of puberty in any young woman can produce unpleasant symptoms, and our girls are certainly no exception to that. I know my own house has had an abundance of hormone fluctuation as evidenced by saltiness, sleepiness, and the occasional acne outbreak." Hope rolled her eyes and the girls, and the parents allowed themselves a privy laugh. "But you are different than those typical teenagers who only have to worry about cramps and armpit hair. As your estrogen levels began to climb," she spoke directly to the girls in the audience now, "readying you ladies for womanhood, so did the levels of chromium in your blood. Chromium is a mineral we absorb through the foods we eat that are grown underground. It's present in the soil and leeches into the roots and when we eat it, it becomes part of the components in our blood. It is useful and healthy in moderate amounts. However, your bodies seem to have mutated this safe amount of metal and indeed are creating their own organic reserves. The problem with this development is that the human body is not built to withstand such an overload of heavy metal without internal damage. Multiple organ failure is the end result of this deviation, and while the dialysis is buying us time, we cannot rely on it to sustain us indefinitely. The girls who are in critical condition as well as the rest of our girls," she braced herself for the next words, "Are terminal."

Those girls who sat in wheelchairs, too weak to get around under their own power anymore, stared straight ahead, attentive and resigned. This was not news to them; they had the same calm awareness that they had possessed since birth. And the parents in the group sat stoically accepting as well. Some reached a handout to touch their child, some reached for one another. But all listened…and heard.

"Secondly, in the thirteen years we have had the privilege of learning from your girls, we have found out that they have some truly rare characteristics. They are of course the source of light in your homes, and not just in the way that children are supposed to light up your hearts. These girls, you girls," she gestured to the young people themselves. "You've brought a healing and nurturing energy to everyone around you. Hope's aunt calls it 'soul shine'." A tacit hum emanated from the group. "With this trait, you will lead us through your infirmity as well as what we are about to propose for the group." She paused again. "These beautiful young women have been blessed with the psychokinetic ability to manipulate things outside their bodies in synchronization with one another. Scientifically, we attribute this to the hyperactive pineal glands. We have evidence of this *power*, if you will, from the videos of their meditation sessions with the Swami Bahrat as well as other instances." The nonverbal feedback from the assembly let Nia know that the group probably had examples of such activity in their individual experiences as well. "They have also thrived despite body temperatures that are consistently and exceptionally colder than typical humans. And finally, it has been uncovered recently that the orientation of the sectoral malformation in the pupils of each of their blue eyes is an indicator of either a positive or a negative charge." The girls all looked at one another to confirm what their doctor was declaring. "This discovery has led us to examine them in groups where they are situated next to one another in alternating positive/negative patterns, essentially giving them the ability to generate their own magnetic field. We believe that it is the copious amounts of chromium they produce that enables this phenomenon." The group was quiet and receptive, and Nia began to feel more at ease with the positive energy they were emitting.

"So finally, what is the reason for all these deviations, all these abnormalities that our girls alone possess? And what does this all mean for the future?" She went on, "We believe that these adaptations are a direct result of the fallout exposure that every parent of these young women experienced after the great bombs were detonated nearly fourteen years ago. Furthermore, we believe that they are humankind's one hope of repairing the damage done to the Earth by those same bombs. My colleague Dr. Claudia Dereksen and her team at Oxford University, as well as scientists around the globe, have been trying to restore the Earth's magnetic field and close the fissure produced by the attacks because of the potential threat of a mega-solar storm predicted to destroy the planet. That potential environmental threat is now an imminent one. The Earth's defenses will not be enough to shield us from the sun's radiation at the height of this year's winter solstice. Heliodynamics are predicting a solar storm that, without the proper strength of magnetism protecting our planet, will incinerate us. Until the latest developments with our children, the scientific teams attempting to find a solution have failed, even with all the world's resources available to them. Their trials and research were seemingly missing a conscious element. No machine cares if the Earth is broken and no machine cares if the Earth is fixed. But we do. We want to go on...here, on this planet. And with the help of the Cold Daughters we may have the opportunity to do just that."

The explanation of the Solstice Project continued with the parents and children quizzing Nia and the Swami on procedure and timetable. The discussion went on for hours until every question was answered, and every aspect of the proposition explored. When Nia was certain that no one's concerns were left unaddressed, she prepared to dismiss the group with the task of deliberation on the proposal. "I know this is a lot of information to absorb all at once and I know this is arguably the hardest decision we will have to make. That is why we will not further involve our children in the Solstice Project unless we are all in agreement that it is our only course of action. To that end, I will leave you to reflect on everything. Unfortunately, we don't have long. I will need your responses by the end of this week. The Board of Directors is demanding to know what is going on within our group and out of respect for them and all their amazing support over the years as well as the sensitive timing, we cannot wait."

Hope nudged her from behind, "Mom, what if we already know our answer?"

Nia turned to quiet her daughter with a stern glance. "Hope, this is not something everyone can just decide in one day." A rustling grew behind her back and she turned to face the group again.

"We want to go ahead." said Defi's father as Defi herself nodded, smiling.

"Yes. I am also ready." volunteered Elouise.

"We support her." her parents chimed in. And one by one, every mother, father and child present in the room consented without hesitation.

The last to speak was Diana's father who offered this. "My daughter is upstairs in intensive care, dying. And for what? We must go forward with this experiment. This is their purpose. It's too late for my girl. But she will not die in vain if her sisters can make this happen. I know Diana would volunteer if she could. Dr. Nia, I consent. Please help them do this."

She felt as if her heart would explode from gratitude. She looked back at Hope to see her glowing like never before. Breathing in all the collective selflessness and love, Nia conceded to move forward. They applauded and congratulated themselves sharing tears of joy and of hope. She quieted the ruckus, "Ok, ok. Now we must discuss one more element of this plan. Obviously, not every girl remains healthy enough to participate. And as such we must draw the line at anyone already in treatment." The girls in wheelchairs moaned. "I'm sorry ladies, we must have the most able-bodied if we are going to succeed."

"May we assist as we are able, Dr. Nia?" Darah asked.

"I will take all the positive energy you have to spare in guiding the meditation, Darah." the Swami interjected. "Send them to me, Nia. Anyone unable to go but able to gather in collective consciousness."

Nodding, Nia concurred, “Thank you, Swami. For those who would take an active part, we must have an even amount for the polarity to work. Dr. Dereksen has calculated one hundred forty-four spots to be occupied. We must draw lots to fairly choose who will go. Once we’ve presented to the board, we will hold a lottery of the children that remain well enough to participate. If their polarity is compatible, those girls will be included in the project.” With the group in agreement of the conditions, Nia introduced Barrett to them and presented the idea of recording the ladies’ individual stories as a matter of record for future generations. She informed them that she would create a consent document to include all aspects of the project and any images or information shared in the bios and would email each family a copy to be signed and returned. Once she had them all, she’d call a board meeting and present their plan. She cautioned them about the dangers of sharing anything about the operation with anyone outside the room and warned them that until they were in the process of actually completing the project itself, they could be thwarted by unknown factions. Because discretion was of the utmost importance to protect the girls and the project, the group agreed to sequester in the Institute and the family houses on its campus. A solid pact was agreed upon and the group dispersed to arrange their lodging for the night.

~

Barrett laid his bag down in a chair in Nia’s office and she checked her computer. All the consents were signed and returned; they could start to work. Nia gave Barrett access to the files on all the girls including the coroner’s reports on the twenty-one infants who were killed just after they were born. He scrolled through the count of over two hundred subjects and shook his head. “What?” Nia asked.

“This is just data.”

"Yes."

"I don't just want information. I want their stories."

"What do you mean? This is where they were born and bits about their families."

Reading from a chart, "Patient, Vania Dev-Cosco, born 12/23/2027 in West Nusa Tenggara to native parents. Abandoned in hospital after delivery. Fostered by Angela and James Cosco, Stuart Park, NT, Australia."

"That's her biographical information, Barrett."

"But that's not her. I'll take this stuff down but I want to *talk* to the girls. Really find out who they are."

"I *really* don't have time to introduce you to every one of the Cold Daughters. I thought you could get what you need from the records."

"You don't have to do a thing. I will find my way to each of them. I won't get in your way, I promise, Nia. Please let me do this my way. I want to do treat this with the respect it deserves."

"It's all you. Go for it. Ask Marjorie if you need anything. I've got a conference call with Claudia first thing and then I'm going to work up a preparation protocol for the girls and their parents."

"Thank you, love." He leapt to her side and planted a hard kiss on her cheek then popped out to engage her assistant.

"Love," she whispered sarcastically after he'd gone and rang Claudia.

"How is it going there this morning, Nia?" her mentor asked.

"It went beautifully with the families yesterday, Claudia."

"Is everyone on board?"

"Unanimously. They've all signed consents. We're there."

"How did Hope react to everything?"

Nia hesitated with a smile, "Claudia, she made me feel so sure of it all. Because *she* is so sure of it all. I can't explain…she was…I just can't."

"I get it. This girl." Claudia was facing her own feelings about risking Hope. She belonged to Ahi and Claudia too. She waffled between the guilt of involving the girls and the certainty that they had chosen her as much as she had them. But if she let herself think about Ahi's final days or Hope not surviving, she wouldn't be able to manage the grief and continue the work. And that just wasn't an option.

"How's Ahi?"

"Good days and bad. She likes the nurses and one of them has shown Joffrey some extra attention."

"What?"

"I know! Ahi is loving it. She would love to make a match of the two of them."

"Oh, speaking of matches," she started the sentence before she was sure if she wanted to tell them. "I bet you'll never guess who's shown *me* some extra attention this week."

"Barrett Davies."

"What? How did you know? He didn't call you, did he?"

"No. He called Ahi."

"What the hell?"

"Settle down, child. Ahi has been routing for you two to get together for years. He couldn't wait to tell her."

"I don't know how I feel about that."

"What's to know? We all love each other and none of us has time to worry about what any of this means. We feel so good that you have someone like Barrett to share the load with, Nia. Life is meant to be shared. Don't overthink it. Just be."

"Ok, professor, can we change the subject? How are the plans for the project coming?"

"I will have the renderings ready to present Monday morning. Make the appointment with the board and I'll be there, ten a.m."

"Yes, ma'am."

"And Nia."

"Yes, ma'am."

"Thank you. Thank you for being our daughter and for sharing Hope with us and for what you are about to do."

"You and Ahi taught me about my place in the human family. You are my people, Claudia. But the world is our people too. We do this for family."

Nia ended the call and buzzed Marjorie to schedule the appointment with the board.

~

To maintain the level of discretion necessary, Barrett had brought no one to assist him with the bios. He simply used his phone to record each young lady as he could. He did not film the girls who were already bedridden and unresponsive but instead gathered pictures and videos from their families. Then he began with the group who had started dialysis. They were more vibrant after their procedures, so he tried to get to them within a few hours of their treatments. Rudi, Farida and Mamie all had songs they wanted to perform. And Pearl, Maeva, Iris, Jade, Corrina and Charity recited their favorite poems. He was getting the kind of personal take he wanted for the project. He wanted the world to know just who these remarkable people were. He felt his soul being nourished by his interaction with these unusual girls and as hopeless as their plight seemed, he couldn't seem to feel that. They radiated life and he was so lucky to be close enough to feel the warmth of that light. He worked tirelessly through Friday night when Hope was the last one to interview. He had purposely saved her for last because he was afraid that even though there hadn't been a sense of doom and gloom from the exercise, he wasn't sure he could expect the same when he was faced with filming Hope for what could be the last time. He was relieved. Her interview was the most amazing experience of the whole mission. She was as solidly determined and bound to her fate as she could be and even more comforting to him than the others had been. They shared a love and loyalty for all the same people after all. She was expecting him to care for them if she was no longer able to do it. He commended her courage and she accepted his pledge to be good to her family. He said his goodbyes to Nia and Hope and left for London to trade places with Claudia and begin editing his work.

Standing in line to board his flight, he got a text from Nia that simply read, "Diana passed away 8:02pm."

~

Claudia had arrived back at the flat just before midnight with her work completed. Not wanting to risk waking her wife, she bunked on the couch in the front parlor for the night. Joffrey and the nurse he fancied woke her accidently when they mistook her for pillows in the dim room before they pulled back the heavy drapes to welcome the morning.

"So sorry, Dr. Claudia," Joffrey pleaded, "We didn't expect to find you out here."

"No, no, Joffrey." She slowly rose and pushed the coverlet off her feet. "None of that now. I came in late and didn't want to disturb the queen."

"The queen is up and feeling like breakfast this morning, Dr. Dereksen." Ahi suddenly appeared in the bedroom doorway in her robe, leaning on a cane for support."

"Let me help you, Dr. Mulpuru," offered the nurse.

"Darling, you must call me Ahi. I am through with all the titles. I am only Ahi now." Turning her attention to her wife, "Rough night, my love?"

"Last night."

"Yes, dear, last night."

"No. It was the last night." The words hung in the air as if they were attached to invisible string. Only the nurse was oblivious to their importance. She waited not knowing what had stopped her patient's forward progress toward the breakfast table.

"Dr. Mulp- sorry, Ahi, are you alright?" she asked.

"Fine, dear. Just waiting for the train whistle to stop blasting in my ears so I can move."

The nurse crinkled her nose with confusion, fearing cognition problems had befallen her patient as she heard no train whistle. But Joffrey and Claudia read the metaphor loud and clear. Joffrey froze looking back and forth between his managers. Claudia reached for him and drew him to the sofa next to her. She patted his hand. “It’s alright, Joffrey. Barrett is coming back to town tonight. I’ve asked him to stay until I return.”

“Barrett’s coming?” Ahi asked with delight. Claudia nodded.

“To stay?” Joffrey asked, less delighted.

“Just until I get back, my friend. He just wants to keep Ahi entertained.”

His great frame softened, and he asked, “But what if…”

“We’ll be fine, Joffrey.” Ahi interjected. “We’ll be just fine.” She allowed herself to be guided toward the kitchen and directed the others in the preparation of breakfast.

The flight arrangements were made for the next morning and Ahi lay on the bed while Claudia packed. They chatted as if she were just attending a seminar or giving a talk somewhere and that she’d be back soon to share all she had learned. The staff gave them complete privacy throughout the day. The morning nurse having been brought up to speed by Joffrey, informed the evening shift of the importance of Claudia’s last night in town.

Barrett arrived in London and called from his flat. He would pack some things and be over early in the morning before Claudia left for the airport. The women shared dinner in their room and left Joffrey on his own in the kitchen. None of them ate much.

The night nurse gently knocked on the bedroom door. “Ahi, will you be wanting me to help you in the bath this evening?”

Before she could answer, Claudia replied to the closed door, "We've got it, dear. We'll ring if we need you."

Ahi's eyebrows smiled before the rest of her face and she climbed out of bed and started for the bathroom. Claudia went before her and ran the bath and gathered the towels. They didn't speak a word, just watched the deep porcelain vessel fill with the steaming water. Ahi handed her a jar of ayurvedic salts to sprinkle in and Claudia added a couple droplets of lavender oil.

Ahi bent to stir the mixture with her hand then rested on the toilet. Claudia turned the water off and led her love to stand while she undressed her. Holding her steady with the familiar gentle strength she had exhibited their whole lives together, Ahi allowed herself to be guided and cared for.

Her whole professional life she had presented this unbreakable, steely tenacity, never yielding, never showing the slightest bit of weakness or vulnerability. But in the quiet of their home, Ahi had always found such comfort and safety in letting Claudia take care of her. She could cry or come apart at the seams or just want pampered and Claudia was so intuitive that she was always ready with a glass of wine or a massage or just the warmth of her embrace to give respite to the warrior. Tonight was no exception.

Ahi stepped carefully into the well of healing water and Claudia knelt at her side and lovingly sponged her wife's back and shoulders, the length of her legs, and holding them above the water's surface one-at-a-time her frail arms. Without a word, she rubbed the soap into a lather and placed her warm, sudsy hands all over Ahi's body. She caressed her neck and made circles on her earlobes with the slick soap. She moved her hands over her scarred chest as if her full breasts remained. She handled her lover as she had in their earliest days together, staring into her black eyes recalling the lust of their youth. The two smiled the coy smiles they'd displayed the night they first made love. Inviting, accepting, wanting. Claudia took Ahi's hand in hers and interlacing their fingers, stretched it open and massaged the palm with her thumbs. Holding her by the wrist, she smoothed the lather up her arm to her shoulder. With her wet, soapy hand free, Ahi reached for her lover, cupping the nape of Claudia's neck and pulling her to her waiting mouth. They kissed, their dripping hands dampening each other's hair. Their eyes closed to the truth, they were young and beautiful and full of life and promise. In that moment as in countless moments they shared before, they were loved and loving and in love.

Bathed in sweet scents and the love of her wife of fifty-eight years, Ahi settled into bed next to her. Claudia waited for her to get in the most comfortable position and then filled in the bed around her. Making sure not to press hard against her low back that was starting to show the subtle shapes of the growing tumors on her vertebrae, she placed a soft pillow between them. They whispered to one another until the pain pills stole Ahi's waking presence. Then Claudia held her sleeping queen, silently crying into the pillow that connected them. She cried and prayed for God to take them both while they slept so that neither of them would be without the other, ever.

Awakening to their reality, Claudia rose before dawn and showered and dressed for the trip. Barrett had arrived and was ready to begin putting the final touches on his assignment and Joffrey was up and ready to drive Claudia to Heathrow. She returned to her wife's side in the bedroom and kissed her awake. "Good morning, my heart."

Ahi squinted and grimaced with the familiar pain she had woken to for months now worsening with every morning. "Are you going?"

"Yes Ahi. Joffrey is taking me to the airport, but Barrett is here already, and the nurse will be here in a couple of hours. Do you need anything before I go?"

"Yes." She struggled to turn herself in the bed and prop herself up to sitting. Claudia moved pillows to help. She reached for a book on the nightstand and opened it where a marker of sorts divided its pages. She carefully removed two long strands of golden, metallic yarn from the book as she quoted from memory what was on the page they marked, "Our favorite people and our favorite stories become so not by any inherent virtue, but because they illustrate something deep in the grain, something unadmitted." She winced with pain but continued, "That's one of Hope's favorites." Her wife watched as she tied the ends of the strands in knots along their lengths creating two identical slipknot bracelets. She handed one off to Claudia and presented her wrist. Claudia took the yarn and slipped it over Ahi's hand and pulled the ends beyond the opposing knots until it fit snuggly. "Thank you, my love. Now, take this one and give it to Hope Darling. Tell her I have mine on and I will wear it for as long as I can. And tell her I said for her to do the same."

Without any further explanation, Claudia produced an embroidered handkerchief from her pocket and wrapped the remaining bracelet securely inside. "I will put it on her myself." She placed her hand on Ahi's face and kissed her. "You know…" her words suddenly seemed worthless and she couldn't form another one.

Ahi kissed her back and said, "Yes. I know."

Claudia left for her flight and Ahi remained in their bed with the scent of her wife in the sheets and pillows.

~

The seventy-seven-year-old scientist flew all night and arrived just a few hours before the board meeting. Nia picked her up at the airport and let her freshen up at the apartment before they went into the institute. They prepped on the way. Finally, after gathering the supporting data from the adjunct testing and in possession of the plans for the project prototypes, Nia and Claudia gathered their courage, took a deep centering breath and entered the private board room on the top floor. They took painstaking care to present every facet of the girls' deteriorating condition, the strengths that the healthier ones still possessed and the details of the proposed project. The doctors concluded their presentation, collapsed their screens and waited patiently for the group to digest all they had offered.

"Dr. Bomani to clarify, what you are proposing is nothing short of human sacrifice." declared one of the suited men at the table.

Claudia intercepted, "I understand why you might come to that conclusion. But we must face some sobering and time-critical facts. These girls are dying. Diana is gone. Indira, Julieth, Euroa, Jinelle, Laniyah, Marritje, Fani, Kemala, Darshana, Nalani, Chandra, Jamira, Elsa, Claudina, Novita, and Sunny have been in intensive care for weeks and Karina, Ada, Kai, Lola, Hazel, Maya, Daisy, and Alice are all on dialysis."

"That's just a fraction of them," argued another member. "You can't make a determination about the whole group based on a fraction of them. We just can't speculate like that."

"It's roughly a third of the children so far." Nia pleaded, "Ladies and gentlemen, you know I have a vested interest in this group. I've made no secret of the fact that I am not only the lead geneticist in this research, I am also one of the mothers of these amazing young people. I have everything to lose no matter what. If we do not allow the girls to proceed with the project, there is no hope for our planet to survive the solar storm predicted at this year's solstice. All will be lost. And if we do allow them to help, I may lose my own daughter in the process. And if the sun does not destroy us, Hope will die of multiple organ failure second to the chromium toxicity." She spoke with all the composure she could muster under the circumstances. She heard the words as they passed from her brain to her lips and out into the room where she watched as optimism lay flat in front of her board of directors. "Indeed, every one of their families stands to lose everything. But they have all been informed of the importance of this sacrifice."

"And?"

"And they have all agreed to make it." She presented the group with the consents that all the parents of the girls had read and signed. "We are convinced that this is the reason these girls were sent to us."

"There is still a human rights question here," harped the Chairman of the Board. "These young women are of age to decide for themselves, what their fate should be. What about their consent?"

Within a heartbeat of the query, the locked doors to the room were quietly and keylessly opened and scores of the most mesmerizing young women the world would ever know entered, wafting in like smoke to fill the space around the conference table. With the newly infirmed pushed to the front of the room in their wheelchairs, in congress they reached for one another's hands. The entirety of the healthiest remaining Cold Daughters collected in resolute solidarity. Abelina of Timor began, "We come before you with the full knowledge of what we are about to do. We were born of war, but our hearts and minds have been seeking peace our whole lives. Doctors Bomani and Dereksen have been our champions and protectors and we believe that our lives were entrusted to them even before we were born. Our individual cultures all share the same stories about change and rebirth. It is our collective belief that our uniqueness is evidence of the fact that we must be the instruments for this mythical event which will restore the wholeness of our Earth, this solstice. We acknowledge the risks and volunteer for the project with a full understanding of what we stand to lose. You have our consent, but you do not have time for arguing. We have forty-nine days until the winter solstice. Please do not stand in the way of our destiny."

A subtle but palpable wave of amity overtook the room as the girls and their benefactors exchanged eye contact. The unconscious comprehension and direction of this plan was understood by all and opposed by none.

The board granted the faction full use of the institute and began arranging the necessary auxiliary support needed to execute the project. A letter of urgent need was conveyed to the Secretary of the United Coalition who had remained a proponent of the scientific solutions in spite of the complex global controversy, and a sealed executive order was awarded the clandestine plan. A covert installation was set up by Black Ops forces on the beaches of the northern outlet of the channel between the Bathurst and Tiwi islands. Temporary housing for the girls and their families were constructed as well as laboratories and a giant hangar where the construction crews began building the apparatus'.

At the institute, the death toll was rising as was the number of girls too ill to participate. Nia watched Hope incessantly for signs of toxicity in between tending to the sick and comforting the families of the deceased.

Claudia labored on to the north in the laboratory, consulting with the architects who were constructing the machines. The teams worked day and night, each shift performing seamlessly to build the M.A.G.N.E.T.S. with exact precision. There would be no room for error. She retired to quarters shared with other scientists when she needed sleep and food or to take a call from home with updates on Ahi. As Ahi's life ebbed, Claudia gained strength and energy. Barrett reported that the pain was more than the medication by mouth could manage and injections were now being administered in between doses to cover it. She was spending most days in bed and eating little. Claudia read the texts and acknowledged receipt but couldn't answer. No one blamed her.

In what amounted to just over a month, the construction was complete. The six submersible contraptions were ready to be launched. Claudia made the call.

"Dr. Bomani." Nia responded.

"Nia, we're ready."

She sat still for a moment alone in her office. She knew she had to move. To answer. To make the next call. But for the moment she just sat still. Claudia gave her the moment. She too did not wish to move.

~

A total of twenty-nine girls had passed on since the project began and another thirty-two were already on dialysis. That left only one hundred fifty-one to fill one hundred forty-four slots. Lab values were assessed of the girls who hadn't yet begun treatment. The tests revealed that four of the girls' chromium levels were just points shy of toxicity, leaving only one hundred forty-seven viable. Hope was among those healthy enough to be included in the lottery. The girls and their families were gathered together and they each placed their names in a hat. The young women assembled in front of their mothers and fathers and Idesah from Surabaya, one of the last four to be excluded volunteered to draw the lots. One by one, a running tally of each one chosen, and her charge were recorded by Nia's trusted assistant, Marjorie. The parents had little to hope for either way, their daughters either risked death at the bottom of the sea or were doomed to perish in a hospital room. But the girls were anxious to be chosen. It was their fate and they all wanted an active part. Nia was torn between relief and anxiety with every name called that wasn't Hope's. But the collective energy of this amazing group began to work its magic and an aura of peace descended on the gathering.

The count continued until there were only four girls remaining. Desi, Marnie, Audra and Hope. The next name was drawn. "Marnie." Her name was recorded and her polarity cross referenced.

"Wait." Marjorie interjected. "Marnie's positive." The group waited. "We need seventy-two positive and seventy-two negative for the polarity to work."

"And what are our totals?" Nia prompted.

"We have seventy-two positive and seventy-one negative. The last girl needs to be negative."

Nia scanned the eyes of the remaining children. Audra and Desi's eyes were wide with anticipation and she could plainly see how perfectly vertical their sectoral abnormalities stood in stark contrast to Hope's horizontal orientation. Her heart rolled over in her chest and she swallowed hard.

Fate had chosen.

"Double check, Marjorie. But I think Hope is the odd man out." An audible breath came from every parent's deepest, most sincere empathy. The girls embraced one another, and their silent support and acceptance sent a current of the same throughout the crowd. All who could comfortably travel would depart in the morning.

At dawn, the girls and their families were quietly bused to Essendon Field, a few miles north of the institute. They flew to the Pularumpi Airport on Big Tiwi Island. A caravan of shuttles took them to the northern-most tip of the island, some twenty-seven kilometers away. The last bit of their short journey through the desert-like terrain of the small land mass offered little relief from the flat view, save the steady steep rise of a ridge pressing up in the center of the island. They arrived at their destination and there, on a once deserted beach, were the housing units and laboratories and other structures accommodating central control and the communications systems. At the far end of the compound stood the huge hangar where the M.A.G.N.E.T.S. themselves were constructed and sat ready to go.

The group would arrive just four days ahead of the solstice and the girls spent the bulk of those last four days with the prep teams, getting instructions, adjusting their suits and practicing the protocol for the experiment. In the evenings, they were afforded time with their families to share what was left of their lives together. They engaged in the little rituals that threaded through their family life; playing cards and trivia games, singing songs, and taking photos…lots of photos!

The scientists calculated barring any unforeseen malfunction, the machines were fully capable of protecting the girls and returning them to the ocean's surface unharmed. What was not apparent was whether or not the energy they would be expending would exhaust their health in the process.

The Cold Daughters expressed neither hope nor dread, allaying the worst of their families' fears. As the days ticked off, the entire operation was immersed in the patient courage of these unique young women. The serenity they displayed was reflected by everyone involved from the Black Ops squadrons employed to airdrop the M.A.G.N.E.T.S. to the scientific teams charged with remotely operating them.

After the second day of preparation, Claudia announced to her crew and the entirety of the island installment that she would depart the next day for United Coalition Headquarters to alert the world to their plans. The girls gathered around her after she signed off to her team and each one thanked and praised her for her hard work and support. That evening, she had a private dinner with Hope and Nia and spent a long time afterward in their yurt preparing her heart to leave.

"I'm flying into Oxford to check in at home first then the next day I'll take the train to the coalition assembly as the project takes off. They can't stop us if we've already begun before we tell'em."

"Have you talked to Barrett?" Nia asked.

"We spoke this morning." Nia and Hope waited. "She's comfortable." No one could say anything else for a moment. Then Claudia remembered the yarn. "Oh! I almost forgot. Oh God, she would never have forgiven me." She pulled the handkerchief from her pocket and holding it in one hand, gently unwrapped the scrap of string. "This is for you, Hope." She stretched it over the girl's wrist and pulled it to fit as she had with Ahi's. "Ahi said to tell you, she would wear hers for as long as she could and that she wanted you to do the same."

The teen's face became luminous in the dim light of their room and she reached for her aging Godmother. The two held on to one another like interlocking pieces of a bizarre puzzle. Nia glowed too, with the love and adoration for the women in her life. The moment remained between them, freezing the time that was trying to ebb away from them all.

Claudia departed the next morning and endured the long flight home. Joffrey met her at the airport and drove her to the flat. Barrett sat vigilant at Ahi's bedside and Joffrey's nurse recorded details on a clipboard near the faint morning light coming in between the mostly drawn drapes. Claudia stood at the foot of the bed and stared at the quieted body of her love. She watched as the covers only slightly rose and fell. Barrett stood and kissed Claudia's cheek then motioned for the others to follow him out. Claudia waited until the door latched shut then kicked off her shoes and climbed onto the bed next to her wife. She rested her hand upon Ahi's heart to feel it faintly beating, ever weaker and fell deeply and soundly asleep.

~

The girls completed their final day of training with a small celebration in the mess hall after dinner to show love and appreciation for all the staff and crew responsible for their comfort and care throughout the project. Nia was heralded as their defender and champion and they dispersed to spend their last night with their parents.

Nia and Hope readied for bed and lay close, facing one another. They had spent so many nights like this, two beautifully strange girls meant for each other, each one destined to be the love of the other's life. Nia spoke first, "I want to tell you something, Hope."

"Of course you do." Hope smirked.

"It's not a good-bye speech or anything." Nia met Hope's flippant tone and continued. "I want to tell you about my family…about *my* mother." Hope's mystical eyes widened. "I was born in Tanzania."

"In Africa." Hope checked.

Nia nodded and went on, "My mother and father were poor and uneducated natives of a very small, primitive village. I had an older sister, Zahra. She was just two years older than I. We were alike but we weren't like our parents. They were dark-skinned, black, with dark eyes and nappy black hair. And we were blonde and fair with green eyes. Albinos." She digested the words as she spoke them and checked to make sure they'd stay down before she continued. "Back in those days, in and around Tanzania, the people believed in Black Magic and voodoo. Many strange things were used in casting spells and performing rituals in those practices. Albinos were believed to possess the most magic. Their body parts were valuable to the conjurers for performing voodoo spells and magic." Now measuring Hope's reaction, Nia paused.

"Mom," Hope interrupted, "you don't have to tell me this if it's too painful."

"I want you to know." The teen settled in.

"The priests and shaman would pay thousands of euros for a limb or an eye from an albino child. Men would come into the homes of children while they slept and cut off their hands or feet. If the parents resisted, they could be wounded too. Sometimes they would just kidnap the child and harvest what they wanted in the bush and leave the remains for the wild dogs." She stopped. It was so long ago and now she was seeing it in all its horror again. "Even though the law had started to crack down on the practice, investigating and prosecuting people, some still risked capture for the money." She sighed. "My sister was taken one night." Hope's heart broke and she reached for her mother's hands. "She was six, and she was taken from our bed while I slept next to her. We were holding each other. They pulled her right out of my arms. My parents lay on the mat next to ours and they didn't stir when Zahra cried out. I was too young to understand what was happening, but my mother grabbed me up and held my mouth to hush my crying."

"Did they know?"

"My father made the deal with his brothers for half of what they'd get. They wanted us both, but my mother pleaded with them to leave her one daughter. She couldn't choose so they agreed to just take the first one they could grab. Zahra lay closest to the door that night. Within a few days the authorities found her remains and my uncles were arrested for the murder. He implicated my parents and they were taken away. I was removed from my village and placed in a guarded compound with other albino children in a neighboring village. Most of the other children had lost limbs to actual attacks. There were only a few as lucky as I was to have escaped without physical harm."

"But the psychological harm, Mom."

Smiling at her daughter's emotional intelligence, Nia resolved, "I was sponsored by an amazing charity that provided me with therapy and educational opportunities that led me to Oxford and Aunt Claudia and Ahi and success at the institute and then…you." The mother and daughter breathed healing into one another's souls in the next moments, sharing grateful hearts and emanating love and forgiveness. "So I have no bitterness, no regrets. And I carry the memory of my sweet Zahra everywhere I go."

"I'm so glad you told me. But why did you wait until now?"

"Because you have shared nothing but light with me since I

first laid eyes on you. And you've done nothing to misuse the gifts you've been given. And I guess I still harbored some shame about the depravity of my people. And I just didn't ever want you to see any of that black-heartedness in me."

Hope drew her mother's hands close to her chest and squeezed. "You are my only love. I was as lost and separate as you were, Mom. There has never been anyone closer to the light than you. I would never judge those poor people or you. You had to survive and make it to me. That was your destiny."

As did every family gathered in the compound that night, the two lay awake for hours longer exchanging stories and preparing for the most monumental one of their lives.

The Solstice

Big Tiwi Island, Australia

The sun shone on the remnants of high tide at 3:30pm Australian Central Standard Time, December 21, 2040, the afternoon before the solstice. The Cold Daughters kissed their parents goodbye and entered the hangar. No tears fell. Love and calm prevailed. Nia squeezed the golden yarn around Hope's wrist, kissed her hands, held her close and whispered, "Happy Birthday, Hope Darling. I love you more and more, always and all ways."

"Four corners." Hope whispered back. Her mother held the teen's face in her hands and sweetly kissed her chin, both cheeks and forehead and waited. "Mwah kiss." The two pressed their faces together for one final, quiet, "Mwwwwaaaahh." Then the girl turned away to join her sisters.

The group of parents dispersed, some returning to their yurts, others taking their frail daughters to command central to take part in the meditation with the swami. Nia was the last to leave, watching until the final glimpse of her exceptional daughter was extinguished by the closing metal doors. She placed her hand on the cold hangar listening to a muffled, tinny din coming from within. But then as if the wind had shifted on purpose, her ears were filled with the sounds of the surf. She turned away from the buildings and the makeshift camp, dropped her cell phone on the ground, stomped her heel through it, hoisted her backpack onto her shoulders and began to hike into the brush toward higher ground.

Inside the hangar, the crew helped each of the girls into their suits, guided them to their individual chambers in their designated apparatus, and connected them. Check lists were called out, tests of the audio connections, tracking systems, and lights were completed. The young women fearlessly carried on with the preparations as if they were readying themselves for school. The crew was meticulous in finalizing every last step for their safe return. Hope was positioned between Nadia and Jayna and found the openings in either side of her pod to reach her hands through to both the girls. They threaded theirs through as well and took hold, as did the rest of the children, creating the unbroken circle and circuit that would become the power of the Solstice Project. A molded capsule surrounded every coupling of their hands and locked into place to keep them connected in the event that they were rendered unconscious and could no longer stay joined on their own. Hope was acutely aware of the yarn bracelet around her wrist. She felt comforted by it. The gel beads flowed in from the bottom of each capsule, filling the space around their bodies to the seal at the level of their shoulders. The oxygenated, pressurized helmets were securely attached and checked for proper function.

Minus their mentor, Claudia's entire crew, along with representatives from Dr. Stanof's team waited aboard three aircraft carriers at the drop site six hours away. They made preparations to execute the project, track the girls' status and record the changes in the earth's movements and geomagnetic field. From the makeshift airstrip on Bathurst Island just across the channel from the camp, half a dozen cargo helicopters arrived to carry the apparatuses to the drop site. The helicopters would use the carriers to refuel once they'd made the drop and wait atop them to retrieve the machines and return them to base camp after the experiment was over.

With the machines and the passengers ready, the crew commander declared, "all systems go!" and the hangar doors opened. The great trams transporting the six machines rolled out toward the beach. The copters moved in to hover over their cargo and ground crews attached steel cables from their decks to each of the M.A.G.N.E.T.S. then waved them off one at a time. As the last of the six lifted off and was carried over the sea and disappeared beyond the horizon, the crew spread out and began the process of readying the base for their return in what they hoped would be no more than twenty-four hours.

The Swami Bodhi Bahrat gathered the remaining Cold Daughters in the central command, greeted them with a reverent, "Namaste" and donned a headset. An assistant stood by to relay any urgent information to him from the ships' radios. The children and their guru took their places in a circle in the middle of the open room. The group sat hand in hand, mindfully awaiting their leader's guidance for the meditation. He addressed all the Cold Daughters both in the room and via the headset, those in the apparatus, at once and began to lead them into a trance-like state equivalent to a twilight sleep. Their pineal glands had demonstrated a marked increase in activity during sleep and without sedating them completely, this level of consciousness could utilize that increase while still allowing the children to respond and react to emergent situations. "I am here girls with your sisters to guide you through. Let your minds be clear and relaxed." He gave a squeeze to the hands of the girls who flanked him in the circle and began reciting slow and low, "Om Aham Prema…Om Aham Prema…Om Aham Prema". The group gathered around the guru joined in as the Frigus Filiae in the apparatus' received the swami's transmission and returned audio to his headset in chorus, "Om Aham Prema…Om Aham Prema…" They were calling on the energy of the Universe and recognizing their source of divine love.

~

Oxford, England

The nurse administered Ahi's intravenous meds at 6:00am, GMT, December 21, 2040. Barrett and Joffrey had only begun to stir in separate parts of the apartment. Claudia had risen early, as always, showered and dressed and spent the quiet hours of the morning just sitting by her wife's side thinking, remembering, hoping and praying; but for what, she didn't have a clue. A miracle? Two miracles? One hundred forty-four miracles? The end? The beginning? What?

The gray dawn was scrubbing off and Joffrey and Barrett interrupted the silence. It was nearing the time she'd need to leave for the station. She squeezed the yarn around Ahi's wrist and kissed her lips. "Wish me luck, my heart." She embraced Barrett who obediently took her place at the bedside and then she followed Joffrey to the car.

When she arrived at the terminal in Brussels, a car from the Coalition was waiting to get her to the Great Assembly Hall. She watched the city abuzz with midday activity. She wished it was night because the world was so much prettier lit up at night. Somehow the dirt didn't show in the lamplight. She arrived at the hall and was shown to a greenroom.

It was noon on the dot, when she and her fellow panelists were welcomed to the stage and the meeting began. Just thirty minutes later, Dr. Stanof concluded her presentation to the nations assembled and introduced her colleague, "...we've turned to a colleague of mine whose research into the connection between fundamental physics and human consciousness has brought about The Solstice Project. Dr. Claudia Dereksen."

Claudia took the podium at the center of the stage before the screen displaying the title of the project. She looked down at her material and then up beyond the stage lights at the people who filled the room. She felt her soul, her heartbeat, her connection to time and space and every breath of every person alive. She felt Nia and Hope. She felt Ahi. And then she began.

"Thank you Dr. Stanof, will you please proceed with the connection?"

She waited another moment while a quiet murmur coursed through the crowd. The holographic screen appeared to glitch off and on a couple of times, finally coming back to full pixelization when Dr. Stanof signaled to her to proceed.

"Secretary, ladies and gentlemen of the assembly, and all who now watch around the world, I have convened this meeting of our nations today to inform you of the execution of the Solstice Project. With the help of the United Coalition's Communications Division we have just now commandeered transmission of every telecommunications satellite in orbit around the Earth. We are well aware that these proceedings historically were never publicly transmitted live but as this is the rarest of exceptions, we have invited the world inside these chambers today."

A rumble erupted throughout the great hall.

"The plans!" Claudia raised her voice to quiet the crowd, "The plans to repair the damaged sea floor and return the Earth's magnetic protection as Dr. Stanof presented were not made a priority, not agreed upon, not even discussed in these chambers much after their initial presentation as the threat of total destruction has loomed over our heads for nearly fourteen years. You leveraged your economies and your power grabs against your own survival. Your governments, your militaries, even your religious leaders could not or rather *would* not come together to create a solution. So nature pulled ahead of us and has solved this problem on her own. As was reported near the end of the year of the great bombings, a number of strange and unique baby girls were born to parents inhabiting the surviving islands that remained across the sea from the damage to the Banda Arc. They each possessed the same physical abnormalities; an over-active pineal gland and heterochromatic coloring of one blue eye, that blue eye containing a snow white, key-hole pupil. But their defining characteristic was there exceptionally cold internal body temperatures. These baby girls became known as the Frigus Filiae or Cold Daughters."

~

The Cold Daughters continued their meditation throughout the journey to the drop sight. They had reached the state of serenity the swami had hoped for well before they arrived, and the mantra continued to focus and channel the girls' love and energy. Nia hiked on through the early evening hours, further and further away from the beach and all its activity. She concentrated on every step in the darkening, unfamiliar territory. She and Hope had hiked all over Australia and while the terrain hadn't varied much from place to place, she still stayed alert and aware of her surroundings. She carried the new camping light she ordered for Hope's birthday months ago and it threw a wide and intense beam for yards ahead, so she felt safe enough from the unexpected. Still she was careful to listen for sounds of animals that might be bold enough to challenge her, although the coastal wind was loud in her ears. It all served to occupy her mind with the task of forward movement and survival; two things she felt certain she would need to practice *hard* going forward.

She watched as a sliver of the moon showed itself at the horizon over her left shoulder and she turned back from where she'd begun to see how far she could see. She was near the top of the gradual grade that crowned the lone ridge on the island. She could see across the channel to the lights illuminating the flat plains they used for the helicopter pads on Bathurst. She could see the well-lit camp at the shore. In front of her, miles of ocean shared both the setting sun's and the rising moon's reflections. She turned away once more and continued toward what higher ground was left.

~

The screen on the stage at the Great Assembly Hall displayed a graphic with the girls' census in the same portions of the ocean as seen on the maps in the previous presentations and Claudia pointed to each island as she spoke, "Two hundred thirty three of these unique children were born to families in Australia, Jakarta, Surabaya, Nusa Tenggara, Timor and Waigeo in December 2027, just eleven months after the attacks. Twenty-one of these infants were murdered by the people in their communities who feared their existence as something supernatural. The two-hundred-twelve baby girls who survived were enrolled in studies at the Huffman Children's Research Institute in Victoria, Australia under the skillful guidance of Dr. Nia Bomani. Because of the cultural limitations of some of the peoples of the islands from which these girls originated, many of them were abandoned at the facilities where they were delivered. All said, nearly two-thirds were placed in foster or adoptive families. Dr. Bomani not only studied this group, but she also became the mother of the first Cold Daughter ever born, Hope Darling Bomani." Saying her name filled Claudia with courage. "We followed these children for thirteen years. They were all fortunate enough to live healthy, normal lives with families that loved and cared for them. But the research uncovered indeed many "supernatural" aspects of their physiology."

"Their biological parents were exposed to the fall out of the

Tsar bombs deployed in the attacks recounted by Commander Merle. Along with their girls, they agreed to lend themselves to Dr. Bomani's research. Helium atoms yielded from the detonation of hydrogen, were detected in their reproductive organs. The presence of this atomic element passed on from the parents and a genetic mutation presenting in the girls at the onset of puberty, would combine to create an exceptional condition, unique only to the Cold Daughters. Adding to the rarity of the Frigus Filiae, not one male child was produced by any family in these locations immediately following the attacks."

"Throughout the thousands of hours that these beautiful girls were studied at the Institute, their lives deviated very little from their peers. They grew and developed like any other children with one exception, these amazing people radiated pure peace and love. The families and the communities in which they lived as well as the research staff at the Institute were all affected with their positive energy. They moved through their lives sharing this gift with everyone they encountered. Changing people, changing the damage done by hate and exclusion everywhere they went."

She took a sip of water. "In or around the end of their first decade, these girls' pineal glands reached the highest levels of activity recorded by modern science. This gland in the center of the brain has functions that go beyond our knowledge of the general activities of other regions of the brain. Many cultures around the world regard it as the body's connection to the divine. And in their tenth year, as their test results on this mysterious organ continued to break records, the girls began meditation exercises with the Swami Bodhi Bahrat. In session with the swami, the children were able to tap into the power of this portion of the brain and affect the environment around them. Through collective thought, they demonstrated psychokinesis. They moved things with their minds. This evidence was recorded on video." She turned to watch the dancing hair session on the big screen with the others in the chamber. A low roar stirred the crowd.

"Now I will fast-forward three years, to earlier this year, when the group began to experience the hormonal transformations of puberty and things changed dramatically for the Cold Daughters. They still maintained their peaceful aura but now with their own reproductive glands maturing, a spike in their chromium levels became evident. Our blood contains many trace metals, chromium being one of them normally present. But the Cold Daughters were overproducing this element, a condition of unknown etiology, and many became ill from toxicity. Of the girls remaining in good health, another startling discovery was made. The sectoral abnormality of each of their keyhole pupils, displayed either a horizontal or vertical orientation." She referred to the screen displaying photos of Tasya, Adelia, Nori, and Winda, two horizontal and two vertical.

"Dr. Bomani would prove that the girls whose pupils were vertical would carry a positive charge and those with horizontal deviations would carry a negative one. And when positioned side by side in alternating patterns, the metal in their bloodstreams would create an external magnetism." A thunderous clamber now excited the hall. And Claudia had to shout and wave them quiet. "Please, please, ladies and gentlemen. Can I have quiet in the chamber please. Quiet!"

~

The first apparatus arrived at the drop site and it was gently lowered onto the ocean's surface, floating until all six were placed along their targeted points. Once positioned, the pilots signaled to the carriers to begin the remote operation to sink the machines. The girls were resting in twilight, continuing their mantras as the great mechanisms pitched and popped and uncovered the huge stone weights that would submerge them to the ocean floor. One at a time the apparatus disappeared from the surface and the copters flew off to rest on the ships, refuel and wait.

The water welcomed the young women, surrounding them with life and energy unknown on land. They sunk steadily. The Swami trailed off with their initial mantra with a long and sustained, "Om" then changed to the next which touted the beautiful, abundant, benevolent Earth Mother, claiming her fullest perfection and divinity. "Om Shri Gaia Ma Purnatva Gaia Ma." The girls joined and the mantra was repeated for the duration of their descent. The vibrations of the spirit song could be felt around the beach base and everyone was chanting to themselves in unison with the girls. "Om Shri Gaia Ma Purnatva Gaia Ma."

Nia reached the top of the ridge and sat, warm and sweaty and at peace on her perch overlooking the cove. She drank from her water bottle and wiped her face, then looked at her watch. They'd be at the bottom by now. She began to whisper, "Om Shri Gaia Ma Purnatva Gaia Ma." as she set up her tent and campsite.

~

Claudia managed to calm the crowd and she continued, "We knew that the chromium produced by the girls, bathed in the superfluid helium contributed from the contaminated genes of their parents transformed the antiferromagnetic metal to a ferromagnetic one that could become and remain magnetized in the cold bodies of these unusual teenagers as well as in the depths of the ocean. And further, since the girls also possessed the ability to move things with their minds, if they were used as the catalysts for the remagnetizing of the earth's core, they might also be able to join their consciousness and create movement in the earth's crust to repair the gap left by the bombs, thus restoring the integrity of the planet's defenses against the threat of the solar storms on track to arrive around midmorning, tomorrow, Australian Central Standard Time." She paused to look at her watch. "But in fact, ladies and gentlemen, it is already 9:30pm in the South China Seas. And even as I stand here addressing you, these girls are sitting at the bottom of that body of water along the scar in the earth left by man's war against man." She allowed the next outburst and took the time it afforded her to relax her breathing and gather herself for the final portion of her presentation. When she concluded she would get back to Ahi and wait with her for whatever came next.

~

Joffrey and the hospice nurse sat on one side of Ahi's bed and Barrett on the other. They each had a hand on her, Barrett and Joffrey holding her hands and the nurse resting her palm lightly on top of Ahi's abdomen, silently counting her waning respirations. When she could feel no more, she moved silently around the faithful servant to Ahi's head, felt for a pulse in her neck for three full minutes without looking at either of the men and then put a hand on Joffrey's shoulder. Barrett watched from across the bed, as Joffrey gently rolled the yarn off Ahi's wrist and dutifully replaced it exactly where she had taken it from in the book on the nightstand. The nurse helped the men out of the room and called in the time of death and began the postmortem care of Ahi's body. When she had bathed and redressed her, changed the sheets and removed the soiled linen, she knelt and uttered a private prayer for the departed, a practice she dutifully performed with every patient. She opened the door and allowed Barrett and Joffrey to return to their seats where they stayed in reverent silence with their beloved Ahi to wait for Claudia's return.

~

All six devices landed smoothly on the precipice of the fault left by the Tsar bombs. The pods glowed with an eerie blue-white light that mimicked the girls' eyes. They survived the descent without incident and now their work would truly begin. The next phase of the operations commenced with the remote animation of the M.A.G.N.E.T.S. Each machine began its rotation cycle, increasing rounds per minute at a steady pace until the optimum velocity was reached and then set.

They all remained in verbal chorus with the Swami and their landlocked sisters. Bahrat again changed the mantra, "Om Gum Shreem Maha Lakshmiyei Namaha." The girls answered, "Om Gum Shreem Maha Lakshmiyei Namaha." Indeed, the rhythm of the sea seemed to echo the mantra for the Universe to remove the obstacles, provide abundance, and increase her energy for the completion of this task to save the Earth. The girls tightened their grip on one another, and the magnetic field gained intensity. The molecules of water filling the center of the open rounds were illuminated as the charged field flashed blue and pink and green and gold with kinetic energy. As the girls chanted louder and held tighter, the chromium coursed in their veins. The force was ramping up the production and they were creating more metal with every rotation. The field grew stronger and stronger until a spectacular pillar of sparking hot magnetism erupted from the center of each group of young women, rocking the machines and rattling their bodies in the security of their pods. As the gel beads sloshed and expanded and contracted within their compartments, their bodies vibrated with the forces of nature. The fields that swelled within the center of each round expanded upward beyond their walls and merged into a spiraling cloud of electrons above the devices and were syphoned down into what remained of the Earth's own weakened current deep within the fissure.

From the aircraft carrier on the surface, Dr. Stanof's crew

monitored the meters detecting the magnetic forces. "They've reached it! Every device is registering between 60 and 70 μT! It's working! The core is reactivating!"

The scientists from the Oxford lab were watching the sonographic blips representing each device as well as the vitals of every one of the Frigus Filiae. The girls' heart rates had sped up just a few beats per minute and though their respirations were more frequent and shallow, they were still amply oxygenated. The machines, however, were changing position in minute increments with every few rotations. The hope was that this was just vibrational and that they'd not migrate too far from the safety of the ridge, but the techs kept calling out the changes as they became evident, "Capricorn, moving 2 cm west. Equinox, moving 4 cm west." If the movement continued, the only way to stop it would be to slow the rotations, but that would lessen the strength of the field and that couldn't happen before the core was completely charged. The crews watched with increasing worry.

With the ocean's surface beginning to react to the violent activity below, the ships were steered a safe distance away from the epicenter. Waves began to swell, and the currents became more and more swift. The giant vessels held their new positions and continued to stand guard over the project as the moon rose higher and higher in the sky. Stanof's crew watched intently for the next page of data to pixelate indicating that the normal geomagnetic field had been restored. Sixty seconds…forty seconds…five, four, three, two, now! A wild cheer erupted on board the ships. They'd done it! The field was restored, and its strength indicated that the girl's power had joined that of the Earth's to once again protect her from the sun's onslaught of flares expected within a matter of hours. A radio signal went out to the basecamp.

The Swami's earpiece was picking up the voices of the girls and also the muffled roar of the swirling water and crackling static of the increasing magnetism commencing outside their pods. He knew their purpose was being fulfilled. He began the final mantra, calling on the essence of the girls' enlightened bodies, speech and minds to harness the universal energy like a thunderbolt that can cut through diamonds and employ the wisdom of their teacher, Mother Earth to engage their supernatural powers and complete their supreme purpose…right now! "Om Ah Hung Vajra Guru Gaia Padma Siddhi Hung!" All the Cold Daughters answered and anchored their souls to the energy necessary to begin the Earth's movement.

At the edge of the fissure there was a deafening roar from deep in the Earth's crust. Tremors shook the girls with the intensity of a low magnitude earthquake. The Capricorn pitched toward the edge and then lurched back. There was a loud crack and suddenly the ground crumbled and fell away from under its anchors. The machine and all twenty-four girls aboard it fell into the molten core. A geyser of steam blasted up from their instant incineration, rising through miles of ocean to the surface.

The Swami's eyes opened wide in horror! "Gaia!" he shrieked. "Om Ah Hung Vajra Guru Gaia Padma Siddhi Hung!" All the girls were calling out from their primal connection, "Om Ah Hung Vajra Guru Gaia Padma Siddhi Hung!"

The celebration on board the carriers was short-lived when the Capricorn's blip disappeared from the screen. "I'm getting flatlines from all the girls on Capricorn," reported one of Claudia's crew. "Oh God, they're gone!" The teams sat in silent shock unable to contemplate the horror. But in the next beat, "It's closing!" Stanof's team began tracking the movement of both sides of the crevice. Unsure of how the movement would commence, they had been anticipating one side moving toward the other. It seemed that both sides were moving at the same rate. This was encouraging as neither wall would have to migrate the entire distance of the gap to create closure. The sea churned above the machines and the crews could only watch and pray for no more casualties.

~

"Ladies and gentlemen!" She had waited long enough. "Ladies and gentlemen!" They quieted. "The project I have just outlined for you is well underway halfway around the world. Six molded polytetrafluoroethylene rounds containing twenty-four individual but interconnected, life-sustaining pods have been deployed to the edge of the fissure below the Weber Deep carrying the Cold Daughters. The Cancer, Capricorn, Equinox, Sunset, Sunrise and Solstice were transported via helicopter to the site of the great rift and delivered to the ocean floor one hundred forty-four of the world's most courageous people. Each young woman with the support of her family volunteered for the mission without hesitation and has left us all humbled by their bravery and self-sacrifice. These beautiful souls are not recruited soldiers or elected public servants. They are thirteen-year-old girls whose uninhibited love of mankind has enabled them to do what no one else among us could."

"The southern hemisphere will be the most vulnerable to damage by the solar flares at around 9:30am, ACST which for us is close to 12:00 midnight tonight. There is nothing we can do but wait to see if our efforts have paid off. Either it will work, or this project too will fail like everything else we've tried to do to keep this terrible end from coming. At the moment of the storm's impact, all video transmission will most likely be knocked out from the intensity of the sun's radiation whether the project is successful or not. So, there will be a static snow and then the screen will blacken. If we are successful, the transmission will resume in a few moments time. If not, God help us." Now she spoke to an eerily quiet chamber. "I encourage you to leave here and return to your families to ride out the wait. We will show you no footage of the operation in progress, nor will we transmit any aftermath scenes. Instead, we will show you the children who are attempting to save your bloody lives. On a continuous loop until the project is completed successfully or not, every screen in every household, business and university will display these unusual heroes. Their names, their places of birth and the apparatus they are sharing with twenty-three of their cold sisters will appear under their beautiful faces. Study them, commit them to memory. They will never come again. Yet what they sacrifice will be ours for as long as we maintain it. Thank you and my God have mercy on us all."

She left the silent hall and exited, stopping to embrace the Secretary and Dr. Stanof for all their efforts. Outside she thought she'd find pandemonium in the streets but instead there was a strange soundless air in the city. Maybe there were sounds but Claudia couldn't hear them. Her soul was spent, and she walked oblivious through the scatterings of moving people, trying to get home to their loved ones or clambering around screens to watch the bios of each of the Frigus Filiae as they played one after the other across the globe. A taxi driver stood by his car disconnected from the rest. And when she approached him, he was moved to ask, "Where to, Madame?"

"Aren't you concerned with getting home to your people?" she asked.

"I have no one."

"You have now. Oxford please." She walked past him and climbed into the front seat with the stranger and the car pulled out onto the vacant street and headed for the coast. They passed a billboard playing the bios. The first of the girls appeared gigantic over the city, *Lestari – Jakarta – Equinox* printed below her amazing brown face. She spoke of her love of her parents who took her in when she was born and of her faith in the project to reset Mother Earth's wellness. A series of shots of Lestari with her older brother and their pets flashed in intervals and then her melodious laughter caught on camera ended her montage. The next one read, *Hasna – Surabaya - Cancer…*

~

Nia lay on her back watching the sky for hours and even drifted off to sleep for a few moments at a time. She noticed as the night wore on that the clear sky had begun to roil with clouds to the northwest. Strange circulating formations billowed out to sea. They seemed to be attracted from every direction and became concentrated well beyond the horizon. She could not know for sure if this was related to the project, but she sensed that the weather was reacting to the turmoil under the open ocean in that direction. She called on her soul to stay calm and only project the white warmth of love toward the girls. She whispered to Hope now, "Om Ah Hung Vajra Guru Gaia Padma Siddhi Hung."

~

The grind of the rocks along the fissure was deafening in the Swami's earpiece but he persevered knowing how much louder it must be to the submerged girls. His chanting increased in volume and intensity. The girls in the room with him were swaying with the energy they were creating for their sisters hundreds of miles away, their love compounding and expanding in the effort. There was a heat generating from the group as they continued their vigil. But below the depths of the South China Sea the water was cold and turbulent.

The ridges of the rift were tracking at about sixty meters an hour, steadily grating toward each other along the ocean floor.

Great chunks of each ridge crumbled and rolled into the narrowing gap. Others broke away and pummeled the remaining units perched on the eastern precipice. As the girls clung to one another and their chanting grew in passion and power their vital signs began to reveal the great stress their bodies were under. Technicians called out, "Six girls aboard Cancer are showing rapidly decreasing blood pressures…now eight…now eleven!" Another tech, "Reporting the same for Sunset, fourteen total, near critical levels." The medical team on board the carrier reviewed the data, "They're bleeding out." Random capsules throughout the swirling rounds were dotting with dark red fluid seeping from the suits of the meditating girls into the gel beads that filled their pods. "The magnetic field must be drawing the chromium out of their bodies. They'll be shredded from the inside out!" The staff could only watch in horror as they calculated what maximum risk could be afforded before aborting.

Another horrific crack from under Sunrise and the machine was rammed from underneath by a jutting blade of rock thrusting it up and into Solstice. The two rounds collided in a revolving crash and broke apart filling the pods with sea water and crushing the girls in the wreckage. The bodies of the lifeless children were trapped inside the twisted mechanisms or tossed around in the swirling currents and scattered to the depths. Waves of water caught in the inertia of the rounds rocked the other machines. The surface crews reported the losses and remained vigilant for the girls who remained, working through their shock and tears.

Only half the apparatus remained intact now. Seventy-two girls remained in place in their pods but of those, a mere twenty-five aboard the Cancer and Sunset combined were identified as conscious. The girls who could, held tighter to the loosening grips of their dying sisters and called out their mantras with all their hearts, "Om Ah Hung Vajra Guru Gaia Padma Siddhi Hung!"

~

Few people remained on the roadways between Brussels and Calais. The driver weaved through what traffic there was while Claudia calculated the time. They drove past the ferry ports only to find that the entrance to the channel tunnel was shut down.

"Looks like the Chunnel is closed, Madame."

"I don't mind doubling back to take the ferry, sir. But that will add another hour to the trip, correct?"

"Yes, Madame. But if the traffic is anything like this, we should be able to make up the time once we land at Dover."

"That's all I can ask for, sir."

"Henri."

"Henri, I am Claudia."

"It is a pleasure to make your acquaintance."

"Likewise, sir. Will it distract you if I watch from my tablet while you drive?"

"No Madame. I would like to hear about the Cold Daughters too."

"Very well, Henri." She produced the device from her attaché and projected the hologram onto the dashboard of the tiny car. "That's Ermalinda. She's a pill." The screen read that the girl was from Timor and riding on the Solstice. The two travelers smiled and even laughed a little when the girl on the screen told a corny but innocent joke. Her smile was captivating even though her permanent teeth still seemed too big for her delicate mouth, a reminder that these girls were only beginning to grow out of their childhood. The driver and his fare had no way of knowing that this charming beauty was already gone. A dozen more or so and they were almost to the ferry launch. They would pass the time watching more of the bio clips until they made it across the channel to the shores of Dover. Claudia thought about calling home to announce her return and that she was bringing a guest, but she was afraid of knowing what had gone on while she was away. Better to concentrate on the girls. This was her project. Ahi would have wanted to see every face and hear every voice. She would want Claudia to watch them as they graced the screens everywhere.

~

The sun was beginning to rise, and Nia sat up and afforded herself another look at her watch, 6:30am. The final hours were upon them now. She watched as the gray horizon flashed with fury. That was her daughter out there, literally moving heaven and Earth. She grew fearlessly confident and set about stoking the dampened campfire to boil water for her morning tea. She had things to do.

~

The magnetic field grew stronger. Stanof's group reported that the protection the earth needed to weather the storm now just three hours from arriving, was well in place. If they could just hold out for those last hundred and twenty meters of closure, then they could slow the rotations and begin to prep the units for ascent. Suddenly a warning light appeared on the screen signaling that the Cancer had stopped rotating abruptly. The force of the collision of Sunrise and Solstice had blasted a piece of debris into the rotors of its neighbor, jamming the gears. The spinning machine howled and screeched and violently jerked to a halt. An engineer belonging to Stanof's group calculated the danger of stopping the rotation outright. "The concussion from instant deceleration of that degree is equivalent to falling two-hundred feet and landing on solid rock. Are you getting anything on those girls?" The med-tech checked every connection to the teens aboard the Cancer and found no sign of life. She simply reported, "Coded vitals on all aboard Cancer." And then there were two.

~

The car pulled up to the flat just beyond the campus and the two entered and made their way to the front door of the apartment. Joffrey opened the door as Claudia reached for the key and in his face, she saw the grief she feared she'd return to. The big man covered her with his enormous arms, and they wept together for their loss. Henri stood a safe distance in the hall beyond and removed his hat and bowed his head and waited. Claudia patted Joffrey free and offered him her handkerchief as she wiped her own tears with her hands and motioned for Henri to enter. Barrett appeared now too and without letting him repeat Joffrey's turn, she pushed Henri into the room and declared, "This is Henri, he will need something to eat. Henri, Barret and Joffrey. Is she in the bedroom?" Barrett nodded and stepped aside to clear her path to her wife.

Claudia entered the darkened room and stood still at the foot of the bed. The air was different than it had been that morning. There was no movement, no energy save her own and that too was different. She moved closer and saw the stone face of Ahi's body and smiled. "How strange we are, my heart. This face, this is not you. I have loved this face for decades, but it is not you. I loved you. I love you. Thank you for all my love, Ahi. And now be free." She covered her giggle with her aging wrinkled hands but felt the light heart of a child setting a captured butterfly loose from her net. She bent to kiss her love goodbye and left the room as she had found it.

When she joined the gathering in the kitchen, she opened her mouth to ask and was beaten to it by Barrett. "She went quietly with this beautiful sense of peace, Claudia." Joffrey and his nurse friend nodded. "It was like she just kept sleeping." He bowed his head and cried, and Claudia wrapped him in a warm, maternal hug.

"Then that's the best we could have hoped for. What a lovely way to cross to the next thing, surrounded by her favorites." She pulled Joffrey into the embrace, "Thank you boys." She smiled and winked at Henri and the nurse. "Now," she started as she broke up the huddle, "why aren't you watching the videos?" The men wiped their faces and blew their noses and prepared for their next directive. "We have until midnight, mates. This isn't a wake it's New Year's Eve. Barrett, get the tele on and the rest of you, let's find some suitable party fare. Joffrey open the wine." The small weird family began preparations for the countdown to oblivion or redemption, whichever came first.

~

Sixty meters of the gap remained and the losses of the girls aboard the four lost apparatus were weighing heavy on the men and women charged with executing the project. A physicist representing the Oxford group took the reins. "People, Dr. Dereksen and Dr. Stanof and all these amazing young girls knew the perils inherent in this project. If we bring the last two apparatus up before the task is complete, the sacrifices made by the others may be in vain. We cannot stop until the gap is closed." A tech from the other team signaled him. "Yes?"

"The gap is continuing to close, doctor. They're still working to finish the job."

"Then we must continue as well. Please, let's not let these girls down. Medical, continue to monitor and announce vital sign changes for each girl. Tech, keep us informed of the measurements as they get closer to completion. And mechanical, stand by to switch gears and get these machines back to the surface as soon as is physically possible."

The crews reset themselves with more focus and determination than ever to see their monumental task through and return the survivors to their families. The submerged teenagers were hanging on for all they had to do the same. Bahrat and the landlocked daughters were ever present and sang the mantras now with the subconscious awareness of the absence of the lost girls. "Om Ah Hung Vajra Guru Gaia Padma Siddhi Hung!" The chant went out strong and fervently but returned increasingly thinner and fainter. Less than an hour separated the moment from the outbreak of radiation expected with the coming of the solstice. Less than an hour for the salvation of the whole world. Less than an hour for four dozen dying thirteen-year-old girls to save all of humanity. Time was no longer an illusion but a commodity of untold value.

~

Nia cleaned her breakfast dishes and stomped out the embers of the morning fire. She thought the position of the sun in the sky read close to zero hour and she looked at her watch to check her calculation. It was 9:10am. In twenty minutes, give or take, she may be seared off the surface of the planet where she sat. Or, she may find herself rescued from that plight by the love of her life. Either way, she had time for one last act of love between her beautiful, odd, exceptional cold daughter and herself. She reached into her backpack and pulled out the tattered, time-worn copy of her daughter's favorite book and began to read, "There once was a tree…and she loved a little boy…"

~

The nurse had not called for an ambulance to remove Ahi to the mortuary. It seemed a moot point and none of the inhabitants of the flat minded at all. They had moved into the parlor to watch the videos and were entranced by the simple and immutable grace of every one of the Cold Daughters. Every feature of their youthful faces was captivating. Their smiles were brighter, their eyes more inviting than ever before. *Dea-Surabaya-Sunrise*, the caption read, and they watched the child on the screen dazzle with a voice like a meadowlark. *Celeste – Waigeo – Capricorn*, read the next. Then came *Ika – Nusa Tengarra – Equinox*, and *Cahya – Jakarta - Sunset* and *Dewi – Jakarta - Cancer*. Barrett enhanced the montages with the occasional footnote from the filming. Claudia remembered them from her visits to the Institute. Joffrey and the nurse sat clinging to each other grateful for the reassuring company. And Henri, grateful for any company, studied the girls in the video as well as the people in the room with him. He had been alone in Brussels but now he faced the end of the world with people who had been touched by such undeniable compassion for one another that he couldn't help feel it too.

~

The Sunset and Equinox held steady to the positions they were in and even though the girls aboard both devices were showing increasing signs of physiological distress, the gap was narrowing more and more with every rotation of the apparatus. Only a few on each device remained conscious and interactive with the swami. The engineers on the surface reported just centimeters to go before complete closure and the whole ship looked at the clock as the last minutes before the storm was due to hit the atmosphere ticked by. Then came one final resounding BOOM! The gap was closed. There was a mad eruption of cheers and congratulations aboard the ship. The scientists and medics shook off the celebrants and redirected the mechanical and technical crews to slow the rotations and prepare the M.A.G.N.E.T.S for recovery.

~

Nia finished reading at 9:30 exactly, “And the tree was happy. The End.” She raised her eyes and looked toward the sea. There was no change in the wind. No sonic boom. No flames in the sky. No smell of scorched earth. A contented smile crept over her face and she sighed. She closed her eyes and lifted her head to the heavens. “Thank you, Universe! Thank you, Mother Earth! Thank you, Hope!” Her heroic daughter and her amazing sisters had done the impossible. “How’s that for extra credit, God?” She fell on her back and was still for a moment longer then sat back up and fixed her gaze on the horizon to wait for the return of her daughter.

~

The clock in the parlor began its first of twelve chimes as the screen crackled with static conquering the video. Bong…Bong…Bong… Barrett reached for Claudia’s hand. Bong…Bong…Bong. Joffrey held the nurse close and she buried her face in his hard chest. Bong…Bong…Bong. Henri folded his hands in prayer. Bong…Bong…Bong… And the screen went black. Ten seconds. Twenty. One full minute passed, and no one breathed. And then the light outline of a figure attempted to immerge from the snowy screen. The video had frozen on the last face. As the static cleared, they could see her timeless beauty caught on tape. It was their own Hope Darling and they sat as captivated with her image as they had the girl herself. The video started and stopped at first until it ran smoothly through to the end. She spoke of the significance of this chance she and the Cold Daughters had to do something so important. She said how honored she was to be Nia’s daughter and to have experienced the love and joy of belonging to her family. And to conclude her segment, she said, “And my Aunt Ahi told me once, ‘No matter how long we are tethered to this place, love and joy are the very best things we can leave behind.’ The caption below her sweet face read, *Hope – Australia – Capricorn.*

ABOUT THE AUTHOR

Diana Johnson grew up in Fairmont, West Virginia not far from where she lives now with her husband and daughter. Experiencing the 1970's in a small town in a rural state, she likens to living in a loaf of white bread. No social upheaval like the 60's, no music television revolution like the 80's and little to no encouragement for a young writer born into an All In The Family archetype. There was no talk of college or anything else really, so she did what her parents did, she graduated high school, married, and started her family straight away.

She began her first attempts at storytelling when she was a young mother outlining novels and screenplays on a used word processor, between T-ball practices and loads of laundry. But she was busy and easily distracted so these works lay incomplete at the bottom of her dresser drawer for years.

Her ignorance was blissful only until around her twenty-eighth year when her prefrontal cortex developed, and she realized that she had made a grave error in judgement. Lucky or not, the legal system would let her divorce her husband of ten years with nothing more than her three sons, a dog, and $600 a month in support.

Then came the "jobs". There was nursing assistant, LPN, sales rep, addiction recovery programs, night shift on the psyche ward at the veteran's hospital, then – BOOM! Kid number four! Yes, twenty years and two husbands later, she gave birth to her daughter and woke up!

She only changed jobs thrice more to become a massage therapist, a kinesiology instructor, and finally an anatomy teacher at the junior college near her home. It wasn't until she was face to face with teaching a math class – A MATH CLASS – that she re-evaluated her life plan and decided to give writing her full attention. Compiling a bank of stories and characters from all her other lives, she began to weave them into her own signature tales of life and love.

That was three years ago. To date she has published this, her debut novel, Cold Daughters, available now from Kindle Direct Publishing on Amazon. As Diana continues to create and craft new stories, you'll want to keep an eye out for her next literary adventure!

Made in the
USA
Lexington, KY